After Surfing Ocean Beach

After Surfing Ocean Beach

~ a novel ~

Mary Soderstrom

SIMON & PIERRE FICTION
A MEMBER OF THE DUNDURN GROUP
TORONTO

Editor: Barry Jowett
Copy-Editor: Andrea Pruss
Design: Jennifer Scott
Printer: Friesens

National Library of Canada Cataloguing in Publication Data

Soderstrom, Mary, 1942-
After surfing Ocean Beach / Mary Soderstrom.

ISBN 1-55002-509-0

I. Title.

PS8587.O415A74 2004 C813'.54 C2004-900456-5

1 2 3 4 5 08 07 06 05 04

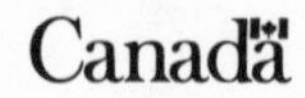

We acknowledge the support of the **Canada Council for the Arts** and the **Ontario Arts Council** for our publishing program. We also acknowledge the financial support of the **Government of Canada** through the **Book Publishing Industry Development Program** and **The Association for the Export of Canadian Books**, and the **Government of Ontario** through the **Ontario Book Publishers Tax Credit** program, and the **Ontario Media Development Corporation**'s **Ontario Book Initiative**.

Care has been taken to trace the ownership of copyright material used in this book. The author and the publisher welcome any information enabling them to rectify any references or credit in subsequent editions.

J. Kirk Howard, President

Printed and bound in Canada.
Printed on recycled paper.

www.dundurn.com

Dundurn Press
8 Market Street
Suite 200
Toronto, Ontario, Canada
M5E 1M6

Gazelle Book Services Limited
White Cross Mills
Hightown, Lancaster, England
LA1 4X5

Dundurn Press
2250 Military Road
Tonawanda NY
U.S.A. 14150

For my sister
Laurie M. Down
1946–2002

~

Rick

~

It is true that I wasn't functioning very well by the time I got to the complex where Lil was going to move. The time between mid-November and New Year's is always busy when you have a restaurant, and that year it was the usual multiplied by ten. So much has happened since then, both in my life and in the world, that all the plans to celebrate the end of the twentieth century seem trivial in retrospect, but at the time the countdown to the millennium was both exciting and one hell of a lot of work.

That's why I was travelling that first weekend in December. It was the only window of time I had to check things out for my stepmother and then help her move. Thanksgiving was safely over — we'd been fully booked all four days of the holiday weekend — and the Christmas and New Year's rush hadn't quite started.

The plan was for me to catch an afternoon flight from Albany, change in Detroit, and then go on to L.A. I'd get an evening flight to San Diego, where I'd rent a car at the airport. Then I'd go by and see Lil at the house. I planned on staying the night in a motel, however. She had invited me to stay with her, but I'd ducked the invitation. After my mother died I never liked staying in the house, and besides, I decided it would be good for Lil and me not to be in each other's pockets. She had made the arrangements for movers, she had file folders of information that she'd photocopied and sent to me, but I knew there'd be some — well, "organizing" is what my wife, Jenny, would call it — for me to do. I didn't want to argue with Lil and then have to sit around in the evening watching television with her.

Don't get me wrong, I would be the first to say that Lil's one hell of a fine woman. My father was lucky when she agreed to marry him. She kept him on his toes and brought him into the 1990s. She didn't take any guff from him, either, which is what he needed, I see now.

What *I* did *not* need that day in December was a snowstorm, but I got one, nevertheless.

Kingston gets mountains of snow every winter, and when people learn that I grew up in California, they ask me why I ever left. I tell them that things are better here than the first place I went after I left the West Coast. My former wife was from Montreal, and she talked me into going there. Big mistake, I always say, but I leave it hanging whether I mean Caroline or Montreal or both.

So that Saturday there was a lot of snow. When I left the house at about 4:00 A.M. an inch already covered the pavement, and by the time Jenny came to the restaurant to take me to the airport at a little after noon the snow was a foot and a half deep where the plows hadn't yet passed.

We live on the same property as my restaurant, Chez Cassis, which means that Jenny and Cassis — our daughter, the restaurant's named after her — only had to drive out to the main road and then turn into the restaurant drive to come pick me up. It should have been a piece of cake, even with the snow.

The guy who plows most of the driveways along this stretch of the highway was asleep at the switch, though. He's a second cousin of Jenny's, and her father, who runs road construction around here, got him the job, but the fool hadn't gotten around to putting his plow on the front of his pickup. He had to spend at least an hour getting it attached, and then it wasn't on right, so he couldn't get it to lower all the way. When Jenny came down the drive in her Jeep, he was stopped halfway, tinkering with the lift bar.

Even that shouldn't have meant a problem: Jenny knows how to drive under winter conditions. We got the Jeep for its four-wheel drive back before SUVs became popular just so she wouldn't have to miss any court dates because of the weather, so she could get into New York or Albany or wherever with no problem. So she took one look at her cousin and another at her watch, and she dropped into four-wheel mode and turned off the drive onto the lawn.

I was at the window so I saw her churn though the snow that the guy had succeeded in pushing up off the drive, but I bent over to pick up my small sports bag, so I didn't see her right wheels slip into the pond in the middle of the lawn. It was filled by the snow, of course, and I guess she must have misjudged where it was, because I know she knew it was there. She's the one who wanted it, actually. She's the one who drew up the landscaping plans, which we'd started to work on the fall before.

When I opened the front door, ready to hop in the Jeep with her and Cassis, I saw her jumping out of the vehicle, which was now listing steeply to starboard. She was yelling at her cousin, and Cassis was standing a couple of feet behind her taking it all in. Jenny is a small woman, but she's dynamite. You don't want to be in her way once she starts going.

Of course, I didn't have my snow boots on, and I'd changed out of my kitchen whites into khakis, a cotton dress shirt, and a lightweight jacket because you don't wear heavy pants and sweaters when you're going to California. I looked for my boots where I thought I'd left them by the door to the kitchen, but they weren't there. The only thing for me to do was wade out in the snow in my running shoes.

Cassis saw me first and started to run toward me, lifting her skinny little legs high as she waded through the snow. She was only eight, and she looked as if she came straight out of those photos of Italian orphans after the Second World War.

"Daddy," Cassis was crying. "Come help Mommy. Come help Mommy." She had a cold, she'd been out of school three days that week, and I didn't like the idea of her out there knee deep in snow. Because Jenny's so often busy with cases and I'm always around, I'm the one who does the medical appointments and earache-in-the-middle-of-the-night duty. I don't mind, I'm pleased to do it, actually. There's some guilt involved in this, Jenny has helped me see: I was far from being a Sensitive New Age Guy when Caroline's boys were this age.

So I raced over to the lawn, took several big steps through the snow, and picked Cassis up. The snow started to come in over the tops of my shoes, and as I turned to head back toward the cleared part of the driveway, I could feel something give in the tendon that holds your kneecap in place. It's happened before; I had arthroscopic surgery on it about ten years ago when I tore it pretty badly, back in the days when I was trying to get away from what I was doing to my life by running marathons.

"Shit," I said aloud. That's not a word I use around Cassis usually. Working in a kitchen you develop a pretty awful vocabulary, but kids imitate everything you do and say so I watch my language when she's within earshot.

"Daddy," she said. "Don't talk like that." She had such a shocked and disappointed expression on her face that I had to smile despite the pain in my knee. I lunged through the snow to take her back to the road edge, and when she was safely in the clear I went back to help the snow removal guy. He'd gotten his blade fixed and was now in the back of his truck getting a cable to attach to his winch so he could pull Jenny's Jeep out.

"No," she was saying. "No, you don't need to do that at all. What I need is for you and Rick to push. Just rock me back and forth a couple of times, and then as soon as the front wheels grab the edge of the pond, I'll be out."

The guy glanced at me as he continued to fiddle with his gear.

"Come on," she said to me. "We need to hustle if you're going to make the plane."

I slapped the guy on his back. "Yeah, come on," I said, and I started to wade out in the snow again.

That early in the year snow is usually sloppy, wet, and heavy, the kind that cakes under your feet. Because the air isn't very cold, it melts quickly and within a couple of minutes you're wet from the outside in. If you're working, you get soaked by sweat from the inside out, too. By the time Jenny's vehicle was out of the hole and headed for the driveway, I was dripping and my feet had begun to ache from the cold. What was worse was the throbbing in my knee.

Jenny leaned over so she could open the door on the passenger's side. "Where's your stuff, big guy? We've got to move," she said.

I watched to make sure Cassis opened the side door and got safely in back while I debated making Jenny swing by the house so I could change my clothes. My larger suitcase was in the back, I'd put it there the night before, and I'd have to either get something out of it or paw through my drawers to find something to put on. But we already were a good half-hour behind schedule, so as I got in and put my small bag at my feet I told Jenny to turn the heat up high. Then I took off my jacket and handed it to Cassis before I fastened my seatbelt. "Hey, sweetheart, put this over the place where the hot air comes out," I said. "Maybe it will dry out."

Jenny's cousin had gotten his rig out of the way, and Jenny roared around him and then off onto the highway. The airport at Albany is about forty-five minutes from Kingston, taking a couple of shortcuts we know and the Thruway for part of the way. However, we got stuck behind a snowplow for a good ten miles, and then when Jenny tried to make up time on the straightaway, she skidded going around a corner and ended up in a snow bank. Getting out was no big deal — Jenny just had to back up — but by the time we got to the airport my nerves were jangled.

The kicker was that the flight was delayed because of the weather. Nothing we could do about that, though. I told Jenny and Cassis to go home after they'd stood around with me for half an hour, as I checked in and tried to get good information about whether I'd make my connections in Detroit and L.A.

Cassis didn't want to go. She always likes airports, but she hates to say goodbye to people. She's a sweetheart that way, she always looks so pathetic. But there was no point, and besides, I really wanted to sit down with a beer and put my leg up. Because by then my knee had really started to hurt.

My shoes were still wet, and I decided that if I could find a nice corner in front of a radiator I could catch my breath, dry out, and keep the knee from progressing to the next stage of pain. The stiff joint was already making me limp a little —

luckily Jenny was so concerned with getting back and finishing the brief she needed for Monday that she didn't notice — and suddenly I felt myself running on empty. After all, I'd put in a good eight hours already that day, standing in the kitchen making sure that stuff was organized so my sous-chef could run the show for the next few days, as well as doing what I usually do on Saturday, which is supervise the prep for the lunch and evening meals.

Suddenly I was hungry. Airport restaurants are terrible. In principle I have nothing to do with them, because they're the opposite of what Jenny and I believe in and are trying to create with Chez Cassis. There are times, however, when a hamburger just calls out to me, and so first I wolfed down two Big Macs, and then I retreated to the bar, where I could nurse a beer in front of the window that looked out over the runways. I dozed off, and woke up after an hour when a great gust of wind blew snow against the window beside to me, rattling the glass in its frame. An elderly couple was standing next to me, looking at the three chairs in which no one was sitting.

"May we sit down?" the man asked me.

"Of course," I said, putting my leg down so the man could pull out the chair on the other side. *Shit*, I said to myself. I could hardly bend my leg.

So it was clear that it was going to be a long, boring, difficult trip even before I got off the ground at Albany. When we finally got to Detroit shortly before midnight, the storm had blown past, leaving huge piles of snow on either side of the runways and what seemed like twenty-five thousand people milling around inside the airport, trying to get connections on the next flights out. Northwest put on a bigger plane for the red-eye to Los Angeles because so many people had had earlier flights cancelled. But getting all the seating sorted out took time, and we didn't get in the air until after midnight, which meant it was about 3:00 A.M. Pacific time when we finally landed in L.A. That was a good eighteen hours since Jenny had picked me up, and maybe twenty-five, twenty-six hours since I'd gone to work Saturday morning.

My bags had been checked through to San Diego, but in Detroit I'd been able to get them pulled so I could pick them up in L.A. since there was no way I was going to make my San Diego flight. I'd reserved a car too, which meant that even though my knee hurt so much I had to hobble to the baggage claim, within forty-five minutes of touching down I was out of the airport and in the little blue Neon rental car, which was all they had left at that hour.

Two hours before dawn, in California again and on the freeway. It wasn't cold, my clothes and shoes had dried out long ago, but I shivered anyway. California has that effect on me.

I was born in California. There are probably 20 million people who can say that now, but when I was growing up there were far, far fewer. In my first grade class, of the twenty-eight students, only five of us were native Californians. Everybody else had come with their parents from somewhere else when the Golden State boomed after the war.

Golden State, that's what all the newspapers called it, what that first grade teacher said when she told us the story about the discovery of gold in the foothills of the Sierra Nevada back in the old days. No irony at all in her voice, in anyone's voice. Almost everyone was convinced that they'd found a heaven on earth. The gold might have been all mined out, but there were ways to make fortunes still, and even ordinary people could live a life of comfort unimagined by many fifteen years previously.

My father was an exception, but then he'd probably be an exception anywhere. He was a surgeon, the son of a surgeon, trained like his father at Stanford. He said occasionally that there were far too many people coming into California. He went further than that: when I was thirteen I heard him say that San Diego was ruined by the war, which changed it from a rather pleasant, sleepy town into a half-grown city full of "poorly educated, over-enthusiastic fools."

We were standing in front of the church, on a hot Sunday in May, and he was talking to one of the scientists who worked at the Naval Electronics Lab, further out on the Point Loma. I remember being scandalized, and looking around to see if anyone had overheard. That wasn't the kind of thing that our teachers or the parents of any of my friends said.

My mother laughed at him. "James never got over being invited to the Bohemian Club," she said. This was before she got sick, when she still was tall and elegant. "He's such a snob." Then she looped her arm through his and smiled. "That's why he married me."

My mother.

But I hadn't come to the coast to think about her.

I turned on the radio and tried to get something loud and pounding to help keep me awake. The drive to San Diego was a good two hours even early on Sunday when there was less traffic than usual. I decided I'd stop around Oceanside on the other side of Camp Pendleton to get something to eat and stretch my legs. Jenny had said she'd call to tell Lil to expect me in the morning, and knowing Lil I decided she'd be looking for me early.

But even the music wasn't enough to keep me awake, I realized as I drove down Interstate 405, heading over to Interstate 5 and the run down the coast to San Diego. The headlights approaching through the fog were disorienting, and my eyes drifted closed twice. It was dangerous to drive like that. I was tired, I was annoyed, I was regretting that I had ever decided to make the trip. I began to think about the uppers I had stowed in the bottom of my shaving kit.

Anybody who's read Anthony Bourdain's books about chefs and cooking knows that a certain percentage of people who work in kitchens are crazy. During the two years when I did the Culinary Institute of America course and the two years after that when I worked in kitchens up and down the Hudson I met quite a few, and got into a couple of altercations with one or two, also. There was a certain amount of cocaine, a lot of alcohol, not as much speed as you'd find among truck drivers: sometimes a bit of chemical help is called for in the kitchen. I was much older than the crews I worked with as a rule, and I had Jenny and Cassis as anchors, so I wasn't as tempted as the other guys. But on the other hand I didn't have the energy the younger ones did, and there were times when I felt the need for an upper or two. So I still had three pills I'd gotten the last time I'd worked in someone else's kitchen. They had shifted to the bottom of the little aspirin bottle I kept for emergencies, and I'd almost thrown them out the last time I refilled it from the thousand-aspirin bottle that Jenny picked up at Price Club.

So there it is, I admit I had them with me in my shaving kit.

But I didn't open the shaving kit, I didn't take even an aspirin, although that might have been good for my knee. It is important for everyone to know that. What happened after was not affected by anything chemical. I was, I am, I have been ever since Jenny took me over, a good citizen, a boy scout, not somebody who gets cranked up on meth or who needs a line of cocaine to wake up in the morning.

So when I came to the interchange south of Laguna Beach, I bought a ten-ounce cup of coffee and a can of Coke at a fast food place and hobbled around the parking lot. Despite the roar of the freeway I imagined I could hear the surf not too far away. Certainly the air was damp with fog and filled with a hint of the smell you find on mornings like this along the beach. My knee hurt — I had trouble getting out of the car, and the first few steps were agony — but something of the peace I always remember from being by the ocean crept into my bones. Yes, being in California did funny things to me, but maybe, I thought, just maybe this trip would be all right. Then I went back to the car, got my small bag out of the back seat, and opened it up next to me so I could fish out the big manila envelope with the papers Lil had sent me.

I continued south making very good time, until I realized that I was going to arrive at Lil's far too early for her to be receiving visitors. However, I had told her I'd look over the complex, and I'd initially thought we might drive up Sunday afternoon. The better plan, I saw, the better plan by far, would be to stop at the complex now. That way I could spend the afternoon making sure that Lil was ready for the movers when they came the next day.

The sky was growing a little lighter off to the east: sunrise would be sometime around 6:00 A.M. I pulled the car over onto the shoulder so I could check where I should turn off the freeway. The brochure from the complex had a map in it, I knew, so I slit the manila envelope open with my penknife, which I'd also retrieved from the bottom of the bag. The directions said to take Highway 78 east toward Escondido from the interchange south of Oceanside, then the San Marcos off-ramp and a couple of county roads that wound around the tops of the hills. That wouldn't be too hard to find, I'd been in that country before, I remembered.

I put the knife back in my pants pocket. I'm sure of that. I'm sure of that because, while I love knives, I have great respect for them. A cook has to. You keep them righteous sharp, you have one in your hand half your waking time, and you are surrounded by people working under pressure who also are cutting and chopping and slicing with instruments just as sharp and strong as yours.

This knife wasn't one I used at work, but it has a connection with Chez Cassis. On that famous trip to Europe that Jenny and I took, when I'd finally decided to take the leap into a new life, she bought it for me. At the time, she thought it might be useful for cooking; we were wrong, but neither of us knew that much then. Without a doubt it was a beautiful knife, however. It was a Laguiole, handmade in a little village in the Massif Central with a handle carved from a cow's horn. It fit the hand perfectly, it closed on itself with a satisfied gasp, the blade kept its edge like the best surgical tool. I used it half a dozen times a day, every day, and every time I thought of Jenny and her faith in me.

So the knife was in my pocket when I drove into the parking lot at the complex and the sun was beginning to rise from behind the mountains to the east. I parked around in the back so I could look at the sunrise on my left and at the complex in front of me and on my right.

One of the things I always forget about Southern California is how high the mountains are. The Sierra Nevada, which form the backbone of the state, are the stars: Mount

Whitney is the highest mountain in the continental U.S., and the long range of granite peaks capture so much moisture from the ocean that everything on their east side is near desert. But the ranges of mountains that run the length of the state not far from the coast are impressive too, especially when you consider that they rise from near sea level. Mount Palomar — the one with the big telescope — is over a mile high. So is Mount Cuyamaca, where we used to go in the wintertime to see the snow.

I don't think you can see either of them from the complex, but what I saw that morning were shadowy, purple-grey cutouts of mountains with the sky pink and orange behind. The Camino Real Care Complex sat on the edge of the valley where the highway ran. I couldn't see the bottom, though, because the low places were still filled with fog. Above, the air seemed more or less clear, although it was tinted with something — smog, maybe. Nevertheless, it was all very pretty, and I sat for several minutes, taking it in.

However, I was there to get a fix on the complex, not the landscape. Lil had written that this place looked the best of all the assisted living facilities she had visited. Built about fifteen years previously, it had forty-five apartments for people who could get around on their own, who only needed help with the housework, two meals a day, and the backup of having staff on the premises twenty-four/seven. The place also had two other levels of care: one for people who needed help with personal stuff like dressing and bathing, and another for those who had to have full-time care.

"As you get more and more ancient you can just go from one level to another," Lil had written. "But not all the people have one foot in the grave. They do a lot of rehabilitation on people after accidents, and I saw quite a few young faces in the dining hall. That should liven the place up, it won't all be bingo and Alzheimer's." She'd added on the phone that there was a liquor store with a good wine selection in a strip mall nearby that made deliveries on telephone orders, "so I can have a drink before dinner and a glass of wine during it."

I laughed at that: my father had always been a good drinker, but he'd stuck to martinis or scotch and soda until Lil took him in hand. She knew wine, and she got him enthusiastic about *grands crus* and small wineries in the Napa Valley and monthly selections from vintage clubs. In return he insisted on a drink of the hard stuff at least once a day, whether at the cocktail hour or earlier in the afternoon.

The apartments were in the two-storey building furthest to my right: they had curtains, some of which were drawn, and individual balconies with patio furniture and window boxes. To the left was a four-storey building, which I guessed held the higher levels of care. In between was a low building that must be administration, the dining hall, and the kitchen. From where I sat I could see the dumpsters for garbage right next to a double door that probably led to the kitchen. I remember thinking it would be good to take a look in there, because you can tell a lot about a place from the kitchen.

A small, dark man came out and threw a couple of garbage bags in the dumpster. Someone in a motorized wheelchair came and headed down a path at the edge of the parking lot. Through the windows of the third floor of the bigger building I could see all the lights snap on inside. Then the sentinel lights set around the parking lot went off.

I checked my watch: slightly before seven o'clock. Too early for an official visit; they'd tell me to come back at a more civilized time if I went around to the main door and introduced myself as Mrs. Lillian Mercer's stepson come to check the place out.

But I had to pee after all that coffee and the Coke, so I said to myself, *I'll go ask if I can use their restroom.* Lil had said she'd told them to expect me sometime before she moved, she'd given us the name of someone who had been very helpful. If I went around and asked for that person I'd seem a little more businesslike, more like someone you'd give the key to the restroom to, whom you wouldn't suspect of planning a crime.

What was the name of the person? I shook the contents of the manila envelope out on the seat beside me. Along with the brochure there were a summary of Lil's investment income, a budget written in her large, careful teacher's handwriting, and the letter in which she'd sent us all the details, including why she had decided she needed more help with living.

Jenny had cried when she read the letter. At that point she hadn't had much experience with seeing the end of life approaching. Her own parents were just beginning to think of retiring — her father is only twelve years older than me. She loved Lil too, and Lil loved her, she's the daughter that Lil never had.

But the letter had the name of Lil's contact, and after Jenny had read it, she'd put it back, still wet with her tears, in the business envelope that it had come in. I fumbled with that envelope, trying to get to it open, but the flap had stuck shut again. To reopen it, I reached in my pocket for my knife and I slit the letter open.

Then I looked up.

A pickup pulled into the lot, followed by a station wagon and a van. Two heavy-set women got out of the wagon and the van and waved to each other. Each was dressed in pale blue scrubs and dark blue windbreakers.

The pickup's license plates were vanity ones: "ANNIE." The woman driving it took a bit longer to collect her things, and when she was out on the asphalt her arms were full of bags of something. She was also heavy, and her voice, when she called to the other two women to come help her, made me think of something that bothered me. Suddenly I was sad, angry, I don't know what. Then one of the other women said something about Christmas before they all went in the building through a door next to the kitchen entrance.

That was when I suddenly found myself shaking uncontrollably.

Oh God, I hate hospitals, I have ever since the three long years it took my mother to die. I thought I had gotten over that, I thought all the times that Jenny had talked me down had been enough to shine a light in those shadows. I did not want to be here, the mention of Christmas made me think of all I should be doing back at home. This was the year that Chez Cassis had made it on the map. It had been featured in *Gourmet*, there'd been a profile about Jenny and me in the *New York Times* "dining out" section, our New Year's Eve celebration had been sold out since November 1.

I should be back home, planning and chopping and stirring and getting ready. I should be working on fulfilling the dream that was Jenny's as much as mine. I was tired, I was God damn exhausted, and here I was, playing the good son for a woman whom I liked, but to whom I really didn't owe much. I was angry, I was furious, I was ... I don't know.

Then the motorcycle roared into the lot as if this were a bad movie with the Hell's Angel taking possession of his turf, the place where payoffs get made. *Oh shit,* I remember thinking. *What is this place? Who works here? How much money has Lil already put into it?*

I had to go over and find out ... I had to ask somebody ... My head had started to hurt, I could hear myself panting and felt my face go red. I opened the car door and I started to stand. The pain shot upward from my knee and I had to grab the roof of the car with my free left hand.

How long did I stand there with my head whirling and my eyes ready to burst out of my head? A minute, two minutes. Long enough for the thug on the motorcycle to see me, to come over, to ... what? I wasn't sure. Settle some kind of account, prey on someone injured, attack ...

He grabbed me, and I thought — I don't know what I thought. I can't remember clearly. It was as if some red curtain fell over me and I had to fight my way out. I still had, I realized, the knife in my right hand. His right hand was on my left shoulder, his jacket had fallen open. I moved forward, I stuck the knife, I stuck my lovely, extremely sharp French knife into him.

He fell to the pavement, and I fell back into the car. For a moment I sat there, looking out the open door at him. He looked up at me. He said, "What the hell? I was only trying to ..."

And I panicked. I admit it, I completely lost it. I was vanquished by all those hours without sleep, all those terrible memories ...

I shut the car door. I started the engine. I drove away.

~

Annie

~

H*e was lying on the pavement, just* lying on the pavement. I thought he'd fallen, maybe. He limped, he had since he was a little kid and he had that accident on the cliffs, and I worried about him still. He was thirty-two years old, but I'd always been more uncertain about him than I had about the girls.

That figures, of course. It was just him and me for such a long time. Him and me against the world, whereas Chuck had always been there for the girls. Bless Chuck.

But of course I didn't even know it was Will when the alarm sounded. I'd been on duty not more than ten, fifteen minutes, so I was still in the staff room, I'd just put down all the bags of Christmas stuff I'd brought and I started going over what had happened during the night with the team head. Sundays are quiet in some ways — you don't schedule baths and physio as a rule, there are no routine medical or dental appointments to get folks ready for — but you never know what might happen. Visitors come and that can be good and bad. Sometimes they help feed the ones who have trouble eating, and sometimes they blow up at you because their mother's socks don't match. You never know, and I'd just as soon not work then. But this was just a couple of weeks before Christmas when we're always trading around time, so that folks can get the days off they want over the holidays. Chuck and I planned to be away from December 27 to

January 16, too, so I was working even more odd shifts than I usually do that time of year.

Will wasn't supposed to be working. When he finally went back to school after knocking around for a while — he drove a truck and was a motorcycle mechanic for my father, among other things — he signed on at the complex to work Saturdays, Sundays, and a couple of overnight shifts during the week. He started out as a cleaner, but because we were very short-handed then and he was quick and careful, he got slotted into an aide's job after a few months even though he didn't have the right training. (I didn't have anything to do with that, swear to God. I had no say in who got promoted or things like that. And I didn't even see him much on the job because our work schedules rarely synched.)

But the spring before he'd got his teaching credential and in the fall he'd been hired to teach second grade, so he stayed on the "call-in" list only as a favour. In fact, he'd worked only two times since September, both times when no one else was available and someone had called in sick at the last minute. That day I didn't even know he was coming in until I saw him on the pavement.

Gus Fraser found him. Gus goes outside every morning to look around and get some fresh air in his motorized chair. He's the one who hit the alarm button on the desk by the front door, and when the team head and I came pounding down the hall to see what was happening, I thought at first he was the one in trouble. He takes chances sometimes, he had a huge argument with the administrator about his morning visits because what would happen if his chair turned over on one of the paths he likes to take along the top of the canyon?

But he was shouting. "Outside. Outside, there's somebody in a pool of blood in the parking lot."

I grabbed the cordless phone unit from the front desk while Doris charged out ahead of me. *Should I call 911 now?* I remember thinking. We're not set up to handle big emergencies, see. We provide backup service, we have trained nurses and a couple of doctors on call, but aside from basic first aid we aren't supposed to do anything that a doctor hasn't told us to do. I couldn't imagine anything terrible happening outside, though. There had been nothing unusual when I came in, the place is a long ways from any place where bad guys hang out.

Doris was already kneeling beside the body when I came up behind her. I couldn't see much, except for long legs in jeans because her back blocked my view. "My God," I heard her say, and I started to dial for help. Whatever had happened was not good.

But when she heard my voice telling the dispatcher that we needed an ambulance right away, she turned around and yelled at me. "No," she said. "Go back in the building and send somebody else out."

"What?" I said once I'd given the information about where the paramedics should come. "Here, let me help," I added, going over and getting ready to kneel next to her.

"No," she said. She stood up and almost pushed me off balance. "No, you don't belong here. Get somebody else to come out."

When I first started working as a practical nurse I might have moved out of the way without thinking. You do that when you're young, when you're inexperienced, when you're not sure you've learned all the stuff you were supposed to. But I've been working in hospitals and nursing homes for more than twenty-five years, and I know I know my stuff. "Oh, come on," I said to Doris. "Don't hog it."

"I mean it," she said. "You don't belong here."

It sounded to me like a challenge, an insult to my competence, and it made me mad. Doris and I had worked together for years, she knew I could be counted on.

So I pushed her aside.

To see my son lying in a pool of blood. His eyes were shut, his head was turned a little as if he were looking toward the complex building. I could not tell if he was breathing, but in the seconds I watched I saw the blood spread outward across the front of his shirt.

I have no recollection of what I did then. If there's any help around, you're not supposed to try to treat a loved one, not in an injury as serious as this. You're too involved, your judgment might be off, you're thinking love and caring and help when you should be running down the possible actions to take and their possible consequences. You need a cool head, a steady hand, a critical eye. Maybe I remembered all that, maybe I just did what Doris told me to do. Whatever, at least they let me ride in the ambulance that took him to the hospital in Vista.

The other time, the time on the cliffs when he was just a little guy, I rode in the ambulance, too, but in the back. It was a very long ride, and he clutched at my hand and I tried to keep out of the way of the medics. I knew something about emergencies, about health care then, and even though he was crying, I was hopeful. He would be all right. We had come this far together, it wouldn't be fair if anything happened to him, now that I was beginning to get it right.

This time I knew more. I knew enough to realize that if he were a patient coming in from outside, the docs would be ready to tell the family to prepare for the worst.

I grew up along the cliffs, that was part of the reason it seemed so wrong that Will was injured there. We bought the house when I was eight, it was one of the first nice ones built along there, but we probably would never have got it if it hadn't been for the housing project at the end of Sunset Cliffs Boulevard. Azure Vista was built as military housing during the war, and navy people were still living there when we moved into our house. The last of them moved out over the next couple of years, and the government sold the property to developers.

But the man who built our house had been slightly ahead of it all. It was a really nice house with a picture window and a circle drive and a two-car garage. My mother noticed it right away when she went wandering around. She'd been looking for a good place that we could afford for a long time, but my dad ran a garage and he had very definite ideas about how much we could pay. The places she liked were all "rich people's" houses, he said, we should have something less pretentious, we couldn't afford more, we'd be poking our heads up higher than we should. But then she found this house, which the builder couldn't sell because of the housing project. She watched it from the time construction started through the year a big real estate agency had it listed until a homemade "for sale" sign appeared. Then she had Dad call and make an offer, which couldn't have been much more than the construction costs.

Like I said, I was eight then, and my brothers were thirteen, fifteen, seventeen, and twenty. I had my own room and the boys shared two bedrooms. There was a patio in back and a big kitchen and a living room with pale carpet that my mother really loved. The only thing wrong with the house was both an advantage and a disadvantage: it sat just across the road from a stretch of cliffs about twenty feet high. To look out the picture window you would think you were right on the water. The cliffs dropped off steeply, with red sandstone terraces spreading out at the bottom. The whole stretch along there is a park now, but then it didn't belong to anybody and we were free to scramble up and down and play in the tide pools and race the waves when they roared in from the middle of the Pacific.

Nothing ever happened to me and my friends, we were old enough to have a little sense, I guess. But the place is not as safe for little kids, and when Will and I moved back in when I started the LVN program, one of the things I tried to teach him was that he wasn't supposed to cross the road unless he had a grown-up with him. Didn't take, obviously, but I guess what matters is all's well that ends well. Aside from the limp, he was okay. He even surfed for a long time.

I say that like surfing was a badge of accomplishment, as if it was some sort of ultimate proof of fitness or skill or well-being or rank. Silly ideas left over from when I was in high school, I suppose; it's strange how they stick to you. Lord knows I've put a lot of that stuff behind me, but there are things that are still there.

Girls didn't surf back then. No, that's not completely true. There were a handful who did: all thin, strong, blonde girls who could handle the big boards, which hadn't yet been replaced by balsa and fibreglass ones. But I wasn't one of them. Girls like me didn't surf, partly because it was too expensive and partly because it just wasn't done. A lot of energy went into avoiding things that weren't done back then.

Chuck says that high schools are all alike — you have the ins and the outs, and the rich and the poor. He says that at his high school the football and basketball players were the stars. He says he knows all about it. Well, maybe, I say, but he is from eastern Kentucky, from a little town on the edge of the Blue Ridge

Mountains. He never took me back there, so I can't say first-hand, but it sounds less like Point Loma than like Alpine or Julian in the Cuyamaca Mountains where Danny and Will and I lived for a while. What I do know is that for a long time the rest of the world looked to the California Coast to find out what was going on, like we were golden kids who cast golden shadows. Precursors, foreshadowers of what would happen elsewhere, as Mrs. Rutherford would have said — maybe did say — in English class.

We went to Point Loma High School, which at that time was full to overflowing with kids born in the years following World War II. There were 547 kids in my graduating class, and about that many in both tenth and eleventh grades too. A pretty big school, housed partly in an old building built back in the 1920s when San Diego started to expand. The original building was torn down a few years ago when everyone got so worried about earthquakes, but back then it sat on the top of the range of hills that formed the Point and protected San Diego Bay. No other building was as tall, and the jet fighters taking off from the naval air station at North Island just skimmed over the top. Teachers had to stop talking when they roared by, and once I remember looking out the windows of Mrs. Rutherford's third-floor class to see a plane level with us. You could actually see the pilot in the cockpit.

This was not the time of a shooting war, of course. Vietnam was just around the corner, and Korea was in the past. But the Cold War was always in the background. Every once in a while as we were growing up there'd be something in the papers about the targets the Soviets would go for in the event of nuclear war, and we were surrounded by them. North Island, the fleet in the Bay, the airport, the aerospace plants, the research facilities:

where we lived and went to school always showed up in those "circles of maximum destruction" that surrounded the targets on the maps the Civil Defense folks put out.

And the town was full of military personnel. When we were thirteen or fourteen, and just beginning to look grown-up, it was kind of fun to have sailors try to pick us up when we were waiting for a ride downtown or something like that. But later we got wary. Not that they were dangerous, they were just outsiders, and we weren't.

When you're sixteen or seventeen or eighteen what matters is what is happening then. Kids like me don't think too far in the future. I expected to have some good times in high school and then go to San Diego City College and then work for a while. I'd get married, I'd be happy. Mrs. Rutherford changed that, though, when she saw that I took physics in my senior year.

Gus Fraser said that he and I were her "equal opportunity" kids. Not equal opportunity as in "civil rights," because we were white as they come, but as in "encouraging some poor kids." My mother would have caterpillared if she heard that, because we definitely weren't poor, we had this nice house and several cars and always more than enough to eat. And Gus's dad did even better than my dad. He was a skilled tool and die maker at Convair, he was the one all the engineers wanted to get when they were making a prototype for a missile or a jet plane, he was at the top of the wage scale, and he worked lots of overtime.

But Point Loma was a school designed for the children of doctors and lawyers and navy officers and corporate executives and rocket scientists. They all expected their kids to go to college, they wanted advanced placement this and enriched that, and they saw that their kids were signed up for all of them, whereas my folks didn't see the point. Office practice and business math, maybe a little Spanish because that way you could talk to customers from Tijuana: yes. But doing three years of a foreign language and biology, chemistry, physics, and math beyond geometry wasn't necessary. For a girl it might not even be desirable.

Gus didn't care what he took as long as he could go surfing when the surf was up. That's why he liked classes on the third floor, because you could see out across the low buildings to the beach. On days when the surf was up, he and his friends left at lunchtime. That meant that he missed a lot of labs and got sent to the vice-principal's office often and just barely got by on the exams.

But he got by, he never flunked flat out, which says a lot about just how smart he was, so I guess it's not so surprising that Mrs. Rutherford pushed him. She pushed me, too, which means that she must have seen something in me that I didn't see myself.

So there I was in physics senior year, on a lab team with Gus and R.J. and some girl who was already talking about going back east to school. I felt out of place, but Gus took it all in stride.

"Hey, man, my mom said you'd be back here this year, but I didn't think we'd have any classes together," Gus said to R.J. as soon as we were told to go over and check out the equipment. "How's your mom doing?"

I didn't know it then, but Gus's mother and R.J.'s mother had been friends for a long time. That was unusual in a stuck-up place like Point Loma where a doctor's wife and a skilled mechanic's wouldn't know each other ordinarily unless they were on the same PTA committee or something like that. But somehow they'd discovered that they both hated housework and liked to drink martinis on the beach in the afternoon, so there was a long period when R.J.'s mother would paint while Gus's mother did horoscopes and the boys would play together.

"She's better," R.J. said. I remembered hearing something about her having breast cancer, and from the way he looked around quickly at me and the other girl, I guessed he didn't want to talk about that. It was bad enough to have cancer, but the very term "breast cancer" was embarrassing.

Our eyes met for just a second. His were lovely grey-green ones, which I'd never noticed when we were younger and we went for a while to the same elementary school. Since then he'd grown, he was a little shorter than Gus but a good five, six inches taller than me. His hair was light brown and cut short, and he was tanned like most of us were at the end of the summer, with the hair on his forearms bleached white. *Yes, very nice looking*, I thought.

The other girl knew him from some country club place she belonged to. "Didn't I meet you last winter at the Kona Kai Christmas dance?" she asked. "Weren't you home from that boys' school up near Ojai?"

His face turned red under his tan. Boys' school? Boys' boarding school? Like I said, Point Loma High had pretensions — and over the years it produced some hotshots, like Dennis Connor, the guy who did those America's Cup races, and Sharon Patrick, who was president of Martha Stewart's empire. When we were there it was considered, if not the best high school in San Diego, then right there at the top of the list. Even folks who had ambitions for their kids sent them to Point Loma and not to private schools, unless they were strong Catholics who might try to remove their kids from temptation by sending them to a parochial school. Or, and this was much rarer, a family going through some kind of crisis might ship a kid off to a boarding school. But to have either happen meant you were really different from everyone else, and nobody wants to be different at that age.

R.J. sort of nodded at the girl. It was a yes, but it was like he didn't want to admit it.

Gus rescued him. "And this is Annie Wallace, she's the one who's going to see that we all get through this course. Annie takes truly excellent notes."

I laughed, because he was kidding me. Last year when we'd been in the same chemistry class he'd copied some of my lab reports, but I hadn't got one of the formulas right so we'd both just barely passed that unit.

The other girl sniffed, like she didn't believe him. "Do you take good notes, too?" Gus asked, putting his arm around her. "If you do, that's terrific. I'll never have to do any work."

"I, I, I, I ..." she tried to say something, but she couldn't get anything out. She wasn't the kind of girl who let anyone copy anything, but I could tell she liked having Gus holding her close to his side. He was cool, he might not go to Kona Kai dances, but in the high school world (which in one sense was all that mattered then) he was legendary. He was the latter-day incarnation of the Great Kahuna, he was the king of Ocean Beach, the prince of Sunset Cliffs.

Later, during those long nights Gus and I talked when I was working the 11:00 P.M. to 7:00 A.M. shift, he told me that his mother had insisted he try to help R.J. out. She didn't ask him to do anything like that very often, so he knew she put a big store on making things easy for R.J. "And besides," he said all those years later, "he was an okay guy."

I thought so too. At that point I didn't do anything more than think it, though, because I was sort of going steady with my brothers' friend Danny. Besides, the talk about private schools and club dances made me feel uncomfortable.

Then the second week R.J. noticed a book of poetry I had on top of my pile of books. The physics teacher was late, and I had dumped the books on my desk to go looking for a pen I'd left in one of the drawers of the lab station. As I turned back to my desk, I caught R.J. flipping through one of the books, a copy of *archie and mehitabal* that I'd found in the library. Poems written by a cockroach, with a refrain — *toujours gai, kid, toujours gai* — that sounded both exciting and exotic, even in those days.

"One of my teachers last year read them in class," R.J. said, handing the book back to me. "Pretty cool. Hope you don't mind if I looked."

"Oh no," I said, looking around to see if anybody else had noticed. I didn't have a reputation for reading a lot, and I didn't particularly want one. "The librarian downtown suggested it, when I told her I liked that record *Word Jazz*. You know the one I mean, Mrs. Rutherford played it in English the first day of school."

We both had her for English, although we weren't in the same class: I'd seen him going in as I was going out.

He nodded, and might have said more, but the physics teacher had suddenly realized that time was passing and started talking about atomic weights. After that sometimes we showed each other what we were reading, but I still went to the movies with Danny.

Until the spring. Until the weekend before Easter vacation when Gus had a party for his eighteenth birthday. His parents were away, off visiting his grandma in Borrego Springs, and he and his brothers had talked them into letting them have a party while they were gone. The place had to be spotless when they got back, there could be no complaints from the neighbours about noise, no underage drinking: you know, the usual list of conditions that parents put down. But Gus and his older brothers knew how to work things their way, so Gus invited everyone he knew. It was going to be, he said, the party of the year.

I said I might go, I even said that Danny, who was twenty-one and legal, might buy some beer. But even when we left my house that night, I wasn't sure I would ask Danny because he might not fit in.

Things started out all right, though. Danny felt good at first because he'd just been hired at a garage nearer to downtown than the one my father owned, where he'd worked before. This garage specialized in custom vehicles, which Danny said was a lot more challenging than the maintenance work on Mom- and Popmobiles that he'd been doing for my dad. "Come on," he said. "I'll go show you where it is before we do anything else."

Well, why not, I thought. It would make him happy, and that could set the tone for the evening. Not that I planned on bringing up the party necessarily, but I knew Danny wouldn't be interested at all if he were feeling put upon.

The garage was still open when we got there — or at least a guy was still at work in one of the bays at the back when we pulled in. Danny turned off the ignition and turned to me. "Want to meet the boss?" he said, sounding more eager than he had for a long time. "He does great work."

I didn't really. I had on a short-sleeved dress. During the day, it had been plenty warm, but now that the sun had set, the idea of standing around, watching some guy poke at the insides of a car while Danny offered a running commentary, sounded boring and cold. But here we were, and I didn't know just how to escape.

"Come on," Danny said, reaching over in front of me to open the car door on my side. "Don't just sit there."

"It's cold," I said.

He looked at me as if I'd said something incredibly stupid. Then he turned so he could root around in the back seat. "Here," he said, pulling a beach towel into the front. "Take this."

He thrust it at me, but I didn't want to take it. "It's all greasy," I said. "It'll get me filthy."

"So then don't take it," he said. "Come on, let's go say hello."

I balled the towel up and dropped in on the floor, but didn't move to get out. He opened the door on his side. "Suit yourself," he said finally. "You can just wait here."

"I think I will," I called after him before I shut the door on my side. But he didn't hear me, or he pretended he didn't hear me. I watched while Danny tapped at the garage window with his keys, and the other guy looked up, then grinned and came over to open the door.

The sky grew steadily darker and more stars appeared. A half-hour passed, at least, then maybe an hour: I couldn't tell because I didn't have a watch. Through the windows in the garage door I could see that Danny was holding a light while the other guy was doing something under the hood. Not once did I see Danny glance back outside. He was making me pay, I decided.

I wanted to leave him there, let him come out and find me missing, listen for the explosion when he found he'd been stood up. I had no wheels, though, and taking the bus home was out of the question. They didn't run this late, and even if they did, it would take two hours and three changes for sure before I got back to Ocean Beach.

Calling one of my brothers or a girlfriend crossed my mind, but at this hour on a Friday night nobody was going to be home, and I had no idea where to track anyone down except at Gus's party. I might call there, but who would I ask for? And how could I ask anyone to trek across town to pick me up?

Then I saw a taxi stand with a telephone in the parking lot at the liquor store across the street. I got out of the car and, hugging myself against the cold, walked across to the entrance to garage. Through the window I saw that Danny was still holding the light while his boss was wiping something clean.

All right for him, I thought. I fished in my purse for paper, then scrawled two words — "gone home" — on the only thing I found, a cash register receipt. I went back to stick it under the windshield wiper of Danny's car.

I didn't realize just how down-at-the-heel the neighbourhood was until I got to the corner. Two laughing men burst out of the door to the liquor store, each carrying big paper bags full of something, as I waited to cross the street. They piled into a car in the parking lot, and a third man, who was at the wheel, shoved the car into reverse so that it squealed backwards before turning and heading out into the street.

The men were Negroes, and I was suddenly frightened — the only black folks I knew were the handful at Point Loma, and I didn't have classes with any of them. There was no taxi at the stand, and what if I called and none could come for a while? And how much would it cost? I had a five-dollar bill, but I'd only been in a taxi twice, once when my mother suddenly took ill at the supermarket and once the day my grandfather died, and both times someone else had paid.

But I was in luck because by the time I'd made it to the stand, a cab pulled up, and the driver opened the door for me and drove away even before I'd told him where I wanted to go. He didn't know the beaches well, though, so he got lost. By the time we made it to Gus's neighbourhood the meter registered $5.35.

"This is all I have," I said to the driver, as I handed over the five-dollar bill. "Wait here and I'll see if I can borrow the rest."

"What the hell ..." he began. "I'd never have come all the way over here if I'd thought you didn't have the fare. No," he said, "you can't get out. You've got to come up with some more."

By then I was on the sidewalk, searching the folks gathered outside the house for familiar faces. There had to be someone I knew. Not that I wanted to go begging, particularly not when I was coming empty-handed. I'd forgotten that you were supposed to bring something to drink, somehow that had been buried under all my irritation with Danny. But everybody seemed to have something with them: a six-pack of beer, a bottle in a brown paper bag, a bola bag that probably contained wine, a big Thermos clinking with ice cubes in some sort of punch.

And from what I could see, I was the only girl alone. Oh, there was a group of girls — five or six, who I knew by sight, but not by name — standing next to the Frasers' little front porch, but they quite clearly had come together, as a group, giving each other protection and courage.

Behind me the taxi driver yelled, "Come back here. You owe me." He was standing beside the cab now, but he leaned in and pressed on the horn. "You owe me."

The clutter of people up ahead turned around almost as one at the sound of horn.

"She owes you what?" a voice said off to the side. It was loud and male and registered as someone I knew, although I was so flustered I couldn't put a name to it.

"My fare," the cabby said. "I picked her up over in Logan Heights and she's short ..." he hesitated, apparently taking the measure of other person "... two bucks."

I whirled around to face the driver. "Two bucks? No, less than that, fifty cents maximum, if you count in a tip," I said, "and giving you a tip after the way you went around Robin Hood's barn to get here ..."

"So he's the Sheriff of Nottingham trying a little extortion? What does that make you, Annie? Maid Marion?" The voice was right next to me, and when I turned I saw that it belonged to R.J. He was fishing in his pockets. "Fifty cents? That's what you want, my man? Here you go." And he threw a handful of change at the cabby, who immediately began to scrabble on the ground. "Now get out of here," R.J. said. "This is a private party."

The driver, red-faced, stood up. "Listen, kid," he said. "I ought to teach you a few manners." But he looked around at the others, standing around, beer bottles in hand, and he thought better of it. He got back in the cab and blasted off down the street toward Naragansett.

"Lucky for him there was nobody coming," R.J. said.

"Lucky for me you were here," I said. I was shivering now, teeth chattering, arms bumpy with gooseflesh.

R.J. looked at me for just a beat longer than necessary. "If you say so," he said finally. Then he noticed how I was shaking. "Come on inside. You'll freeze out here."

Inside it was too hot from too many folks packed into the Frasers' little house. Before we bought our house, we'd lived in one like it: a two-bedroom cottage built before World War II. Gus's folks had bought their home after the war, when his dad went to work for Convair. Over the years Mr. Fraser added on two more bedrooms and a family room to the back of the house so that the lot was nearly filled. But Mrs. Fraser had found room for oranges and grapefruit overgrown with bougainvillea and cup-of-gold vines. Inside, the house was full of heavy-duty overstuffed chairs and sofas. Everything was nicked and scraped from collisions between boys and wood.

Only the tiny bedroom off the entry hall was different. That's where Mrs. Fraser had her horoscope paraphernalia: her charts, her books, her worksheets. She also had a teak desk, and a matching black upholstered office chair was set facing Mr. Fraser's Lazy Boy. They had taken over the room two years before when Gary, Gus's oldest brother, moved out and got married. Gus said his parents didn't cry at Gary's wedding because they were so glad to claim the room.

It was off-limits for the party. The door didn't have a lock, but Gus had taped "Entrance Prohibited" signs all over it, and Jeff, the oldest of his brothers still at home, stationed himself by the door for the first hour or so to warn off folks in search of a little quiet. "My mother would rather you slept in her bed than you messed with her stuff," he said again and again. "I mean, don't go in their bedroom either, but for God's sake stay out of their den."

By the time R.J. led me inside, the living room, kitchen, and the two bedrooms the boys shared were full of folks. Music was blasting from the hi-fi set up near the sliding glass doors, which led to the small deck in back. Folks were dancing out there as well as in the living room. Bottles of various sorts covered the table and counters in the kitchen. Cases already refilling with empties stood along the wall, and cigarette smoke had turned the air grey.

The warmth felt good to me. R.J. told me to wait for him in the hall while he got me something to drink, and I leaned against the wall, getting my bearings. Gus saw me standing there and pushed his way through the mass of people: "Hey, Annie-baby, where's your friend?"

"Which one?" I asked. "Danny couldn't make it, and R.J. just headed that way." I pointed toward the kitchen.

"R.J.? R.J., of course, R.J. But I thought you were coming with your boyfriend."

"If you mean Danny, he decided not to come," I said.

"And R.J.'s getting you something?" Gus grinned. "Ah yes, I understand." He leaned over and gave me a kiss on the cheek. "Good, good. Be nice to the poor guy, life's complicated for him these days."

R.J. came up then, too late to hear what Gus was saying but in time to see the kiss. "Thought you were spreading yourself around," he said to Gus. "Not going to get involved with anybody, no playing favourites."

"Hey, man," Gus said as he stepped backwards. "She has her own stuff going for her, and ..." He took my hand and raised it to his lips like some guy in an old movie. "I'm just one of her many, many admirers." Then he left us alone.

We didn't stay very long at the party. R.J. didn't have a car — he'd walked to the party, he'd always walked to Gus's house ever since he was old enough for his mother to trust him to cross the street safely — so he walked me home, the long way around.

The next morning when I woke up I felt good. At first I had no idea why. It was as if my room was full of low-level excitement the way it was full of filtered light. "Suffused" was one word I thought of. "Glowing" was another. For a moment I lay on my back with my hands spread flat on the tops of my thighs under the covers and took it all in through wide-open eyes.

The house was quiet. Not surprising for a Saturday morning. My brothers were either at work or not up yet, and my mother would be at the supermarket. Even though she had plenty of time to shop for groceries during the week, she liked to be one of the first to hit DeFalco's on Saturdays. The produce was always better then, she said. They kept their best meat for Saturday too.

She would have left things for me to do, but I was in no hurry to do them. I stretched my legs under the sheet and brought my hands up along my belly to my breasts. My nightgown had bunched up as I turned in my sleep so that it was around my waist. I tried to remember what I'd been dreaming about, how I might have moved during my dreams, but I could not. All that remained was the feeling of satisfaction.

Which was related to R.J., I knew. To his seriousness, and his kindness, and his grey-green eyes. To the way he had stood with me on the front steps, leaning toward me and then turning away before he kissed me, as if he thought that he should not attempt anything so quickly.

I found myself running my tongue lightly over my lips. I almost had reached up to kiss him, but I hadn't, out of fear of ... what? Appearing to be more forward, less virtuous than I was? Probably. There was something about him that made me feel out of my depth.

He would not understand parts of me, I was sure. He would not imagine the sorts of things that happened in my dreams — in my daydreams.

I ran my hand down the front of my body, from just above my right breast across my belly to where my legs met in curly hair and secret places whose names I knew but had never said aloud.

Danny had touched me there, as we sat in his car the week before, parked in the driveway at my house. His hand had worked its way slowly up my leg, his fingers had fiddled with the elastic on my underpants. I had shivered and felt ... I don't know. Slippery and yearning, I'd say now, but then I didn't have those words either.

But nothing more than that had happened. Nothing more. I had moved and cried out, and suddenly Danny was sitting up, adjusting his shirt and trousers, mumbling angrily to himself. "Stupid to get involved with somebody's goody-goody sister," I heard him say.

He'd kissed me after that, and pressed me close to him as we stood on the front porch before going in my house. But once inside, once in the family room, with my father asleep on the couch in front of the television and my mother playing cards with my oldest brother and two of his friends, there was nothing more.

I had not been sure if I'd been glad of that. I had not worked out what I would do if he tried again: that had been one of the things in the back of my mind as I sat and waited for him at the garage. One of the things that I would not have admitted.

But all that had changed. I knew now.

I knew also that I ought to get up to do the jobs my mother expected me to do on Saturday mornings: vacuuming, laundry. Slowly, I unfolded myself from the bed and went to stand in front of the window, which looked out onto the side yard. The sun had passed the point where it shone in the window, and the banana palm just outside now cast a green shadow.

Beyond, however, the sun dazzled. I heard the sound of water running, splashing on concrete. Someone was washing a car on this fine morning, someone was cleaning things up.

I turned, pulling off my nightgown as I did, reaching to open my drawer. I was putting on my underpants when I heard somebody bang open the front door.

One of my brothers? My mother home early?

Heavy footsteps crossed the living room and started down the hall. Not one of my brothers, because they would have taken off their shoes before stepping on the wall-to-wall carpet in the living room, and my dad avoided the room period, coming in the back and through the other hallway whenever he could. Strange.

It wasn't until the footsteps turned at the end of the hall and then started toward my room that I even wondered if it might be Danny.

In my bare feet I padded silently over to the door and listened. There was someone outside. Definitely not one of my brothers.

Every one of them would have rattled my doorknob and then barged in. I hated that, I'd been complaining about it since I was nine or so and became aware of the idea that boys shouldn't see girls in their various stages of undress. But my mother had said to keep my door shut, and that was that. Expecting anything more from men and boys was completely beyond hope.

So, the breathing I heard on the other side of the door, and the heat that seemed to come through it, were not coming from someone in the family. Not from someone who might think he had a right to be disagreeable, to bother me, to invade my territory.

And nobody else but Danny knew which room was mine.

I finished pulling on my T-shirt and shorts, and then opened the door a crack.

"Hello," I said.

His hair was standing on end, and he hadn't shaved. His eyes were bloodshot. The smell of something sour — sweat, stale beer, confined spaces — blew toward me. His shirt was rumpled, a long drip of motor oil ran down the right leg of his pants, grease covered his hands.

Grease didn't bother me, grease was something that my father was never able to get out from around his fingernails, something that went with security and a male world that was safe, not threatening. But Danny's smell, his disarray, his urgency disgusted me.

"You ran out on me," he said. His voice was hoarse, and when he opened his mouth his breath stank.

I didn't reply right away. I could feel his edginess just as strongly as I could smell his breath.

"You took off with somebody."

"I called a cab," I said. "I was tired of waiting."

"No, you ran out on me, you went to meet somebody else," he said, pushing the door open and coming into my room. He looked around quickly, and I imagined what he took in: the windows open and the curtains blowing in the light breeze. My single bed still unmade with the pillow punched into the shape I liked, my nightgown sliding off toward the floor. My desk with my school books, my stack of stuffed animals, the dirty clothes overflowing the closet, waiting for me to do the laundry.

"Why did you leave me?" he asked. He reached for my arm with his right hand and for a second I thought he was going to be rough with me. "Why did you do that?"

"Because I got tired of waiting," I repeated, trying to be matter-of-fact. "Simple as that. I'd been sitting in the car for more than an hour and you just kept on doing whatever it was you were doing ..."

"But you knew I'd be out in a few minutes," he said. "You knew that the guy was my boss, you can't just get up and leave when he's asking you to help ..."

"You didn't have to go by," I said. "You dragged me there, and you said you'd be only a minute, and ..."

He was reaching for my other arm now, standing close to me, raising his voice. I turned, trying to twist out of his grasp. At least one of my brothers was probably there, if I called out he would hear. Or the person washing a car nearby would. There was really nothing to be alarmed about, there was someone nearby.

He seemed to realize that his grip might be frightening. "Look," he said, "let's sit down and talk this over. You ran out on me and you went to some surfer party." He pushed me gently toward my bed. For a second we stood next to it. I could feel him trying to decide if he should push me down.

"If you aren't interested in me, I don't see why I shouldn't go where people are," I said. I twisted my shoulders again, making my arms move under his grip. He wasn't being rough with me, he wasn't even holding me very tight, but I didn't like it.

His eyes bored into me. "But I am interested in you," he said. "I love you, for Christ's sake." Then he dropped his hands from my arms and sat down heavily on the bed. He put his elbows on his knees so he could cradle his head in his hands, covering his face. "Oh, Annie," he said, his voice cracking into sobs.

That would have been the time to go to the door and call for my brother, I knew later. No, I knew even then, as I stood listening to him blubber. But I didn't do anything. I merely waited and listened, and then, as his sobs began to splutter to a stop, I sat down next to him even though he still smelled, even though his dirty clothes were disgusting, even though I wanted to have nothing more to do with him.

"Are you going to be all right?" I asked. I wasn't touching him. I knew it would be a mistake to even put out my hand to give him Kleenex from the box I kept by the head of my bed. So I sat.

"Yeah," he said, after a minute. He pulled out a dirty handkerchief, covered with grease too. He blew his nose and then stuffed the handkerchief back into his pocket. He turned toward me and reached up with both his hands to cup my face between them. "I love you," he said again. "I really do." Then he leaned forward and kissed me on the lips.

It was a kiss that started out to be just as innocent as the one that R.J. might have given me the night before: dry, lip to lip, nothing enticing. His breath was awful, and I found myself holding my own breath to keep from smelling his. But it was a long kiss, which took me by surprise with only half a lungful of air. After a few seconds I found myself running out of breath, pulling back, opening my mouth to say, "Whoa, let me breathe."

But his hands held my face next to his, and he slipped his tongue in as soon as my lips parted. I tried to pull air in through my nose, I twisted my head, I brought my hands up to push him away, but he moved closer, tipping me back on the bed so that he was covering me.

What followed was inevitable, I decided afterwards. He was stronger than I was, he was still more than a little drunk, his pride had been hurt. And he loved me after his fashion.

I saw that then, as I saw it later.

Afterwards he was embarrassed and ashamed and afraid I'd tell my brothers. But I had no intention of doing that, because to do so would be to acknowledge that he had a claim on me. As I lay under him, listening to him ask my pardon, waiting for him to let me up, I felt my heart harden. *No*, I told myself, *this is not happening. This does not count. I cannot bear to have it count.*

"Get out of here," I said, when he had finished apologizing. "I don't want to see you ever again," I added, sitting up now that he was off me. "I am going to go down the hall to the bathroom, and I am going to take a shower, and when I come back I want you out of here. Otherwise ..."

I left the threat floating in the air. Then I stood up and walked, my legs shaking, to the bathroom. I shut the door and heaved everything I had eaten for the last twenty-four hours into the toilet. I turned on the shower and waited while the water warmed up, looking at myself in the mirror. My mouth tasted like vomit and Danny's breath, and my skin crawled when I thought of how he had touched me there and there and there.

His footsteps came down the hall, then paused in front of the door. He tapped lightly. "Annie," he said. "I'm sorry ..." I flushed the toilet and pulled back the shower curtain so I could step in. After that, I let the water run and run and run over me. I did not hear whatever he did then.

~

Rick

~

I *made all the right turns driving* to Point Loma from the place where Lil was moving. I even remembered where to pick up the road that takes you over to Interstate 5 at Carlsbad on the coast, but I must have been operating on automatic pilot, following directions that had entered my head more than ten, fifteen years before, the last time I'd been in the North County. Not even the sight of the surf rolling in, glimpsed when the road dipped down by the beach, took me out of the welter of half-formed images and overwhelming fears that had taken possession of me.

I came to my senses where the freeway cuts down Rose Canyon and arrives at Mission Bay. The roads had been rerouted since the last time I was there and I nearly missed the turnoff that takes you across the causeway and onto Sunset Cliffs Boulevard. From there the way was automatic again. But I knew I could not greet Lil until I sat and thought about what I had done.

This early on a December Sunday there were only a few dog walkers on the stretch of the beach where I parked the car. I got out because I still hadn't peed, and as I relieved myself in the sand, shielded from view by the car door, I thought about taking off my shoes and walking on the beach. The sand is very fine here, with grey grains so small that they feel like silk running through your fingers. In the morning light it looked only slightly darker than the water and the remnants of fog that hung over the beach, but I knew that interspersed with grey were enough black grains to intensify the shadows on sunny days. Thinking about it, I could feel how cool the sand would be, how all the bones in my feet would loosen, how I would be anchored to the earth at the place where earth meets sea.

But when I tried to step out, to walk just a bit, my knee screamed at me. I decided I couldn't deal with it and with what had happened at the same time so I retreated back into the car.

This stretch of shoreline is like home to me. I've got four watercolours my mother did of the cliffs a little further south hanging in Chez Cassis. Gus was around while she worked on them, while his mother did her astrological charts. He and I would climb over the rocks where there were tide pools full of anemones and scuttling crabs and long strands of seaweed. We knew where the caves were and where the best anemones were. We'd take sticks and poke them into the centre of their flower-like bodies and dance around when they would contract into stone-like lumps. We'd jump from the edge of the rocks to the soft sand below, we'd find driftwood and try to start fires with matches stolen from our cigarette-smoking mothers.

But the broad beach in front of me with the long line of waves rolling in fascinated my mother, too. I remember hearing her tell my father that it wasn't a waste of her time to lie on the sand and let me build castles, because being connected to the rhythms of the ocean cleansed her body and her spirit. They were big words, which made an impression on a small boy: I must have been aware already at that point that things were not going as they should.

The beach just south of here — Ocean Beach proper — is where Gus took me surfing when I came back to Point Loma from my exile in the boys' school. I'd been away for my sophomore and junior years, and I'd hated it. After I married Caroline and went back east and got to know people who'd grown up there, I discovered that there were schools where academic excellence was considered as important as sports or meeting boys who would form an old boys' network in ten years' time. But the school my parents sent me to wasn't a Western version of Choate or some other Ivy League prep school, nor was it a Jesuit or Christian Brothers school, where there was a centuries-old tradition of dedicated teaching.

No, what they put me in was an imitation military academy, which advertised itself as making men out of boys. There were drills and parades and uniforms and teachers you could only address after saluting and whom you had to call "Sir." There were also a lot of boys who were having problems adjusting to a new stepfather or who had parents who travelled a lot or, as in my case, had death hovering over their families. Some of the boys were cruel, some of them were stupid, none of them came from Point Loma or Ocean Beach, and I had very few friends.

I was bad at everything except the school work (which wasn't very challenging to anyone who could read with ease) and target practice. The school had two rifle ranges: one outside where we used three artillery pieces left over from the First World War as well as .22s; and one underneath the gymnasium where we shot .22s and handguns. I liked the smell there, and the feel of lying on my belly and shooting at a target, with the weapon rebounding against my shoulder, the sudden noise that stopped my breathing, the satisfaction of hitting something far from me with what might be deadly force.

During those years I lived for the summers and holidays, even though the house was heavy with my mother's illness. She had been diagnosed with breast cancer when I was fourteen, but her health problems had begun before that. By the time I was ten, her arthritis had made it hard for her to walk along the shore or carry her easel and watercolours. She tried to ignore her sore and swollen joints — perhaps to protect me — but I didn't mind fetching and carrying what she couldn't handle herself. She was funny, she was cheerful, she was affectionate. None of which my father was.

But then she went into remission and, through one of those quirks that medicine can't explain, the arthritis all but disappeared too. Both she and my father knew that it wouldn't last, but they didn't tell me. They just asked if I wanted to stay in San Diego and do my last year of high school at Point Loma.

I said yes without thinking twice. It couldn't be worse than the boarding school, I told myself when I had a chance to think about what it meant — coming into a place where people had been together for sophomore and junior years already, where I'd have to try to make friends again.

And as it turned out, I knew a lot of people, at least by face or name, because we'd been little kids together. And Gus looked out for me. In return I helped him with lab reports and class notes when he cut too many classes.

"You gotta come surfing, man," he said the Friday after the first physics test, which he'd passed because I filled in the gaps for him. "You spend too much time indoors, you're looking peaked."

"Yeah sure," I said. My father had seen a lot of surfing injuries and he'd always said I'd be a fool if I surfed — both because of the danger and because he would cut off my allowance for being so damn stupid. He was right about the chance of accident, of course: years later, when he was twenty-five, Gus broke his neck, and when my own boys wanted to do snowboarding I was just as adamant about not giving permission as my father had been.

But just as my sons figured out a way to snowboard without me knowing until later, I went surfing too. That first afternoon with Gus I knew nobody was going to check up on me. My parents had gone to Los Angeles to see the galleries, stay at the Beverly Wiltshire, and eat in restaurants featuring something besides prime rib and fried chicken. It was a trip my mother had been planning ever since she had begun her remission, and she arranged with the Mexican woman who cleaned and sometimes cooked so that she would leave something ready for me to eat when I came home. But the woman would not be there.

"Come on. You won't regret it," Gus said, while I considered my options. "You can use my old board, man. Don't worry, you won't get stuck on the beach."

"Oh, it's not that," I said. The girls at the next lockers had gathered their things together and were slamming shut the doors. One of them was watching. "It's just, you know, it's been a long time ..."

I let that hang in the air. The last time Gus and I had gone to the beach together had been just before I went away to school. He'd begun to surf on a board by then, but because I didn't know anything, we did what we'd done when we were little. Back then, we'd paddle around on air mattresses, riding in the waves that broke closest to the shore. Or we'd work our way out as far as the waist-deep water where the waves broke higher than our heads. We'd kick off from the bottom as a swell approached, swimming like hell to keep up with the advancing wave. Then, if we were lucky, the momentum of the wave would surround us as it broke, pushing us forward toward the shore. With our arms pressed against our sides, we'd shoot ahead of the wave, parallel to its movement, with our heads and sometimes our shoulders completely out of the water. The ride would last no longer than ten seconds, but then we'd stand up in the shallows, exhilarated, drunk with the power that we'd been a part of, even for so brief a time.

Surfing felt like that, but multiplied ten, twenty times. And it required much more skill. Until the end of the 1950s no one much under fourteen or fifteen could handle a surfboard because they were all between seven and ten feet long and weighed more than fifty pounds. Once in the water, they were more manoeuvrable, but the out-of-water hassle kept anyone very young from trying.

By the time I came back to Point Loma, though, new shorter, lighter boards had begun to take over. A handful of young guys had had the surf to themselves before, but then the best beaches became busy with boards made out of balsa wood and fibreglass.

Gus was sure I would have no trouble with a short board. "So it's been a long time," he said, slamming shut his locker. "So what? You'll be all right." He turned to go, and there was no question whether I would follow. Ordinarily I took the bus home, but when I reached the bottom of the stairs I turned toward the parking lot with Gus.

In the section nearest the school, fifteen places were reserved for cars being worked on by the guys taking auto shop. Beyond sat perhaps a hundred cars, some belonging to teachers, but at least half belonging to students. Many of these were in very bad shape, but two Thunderbirds carefully parked away from overhanging eucalyptus trees were the property of seniors who'd fished the summer before, Portuguese guys whose families had tuna boats and who could clear several thousand dollars on one fishing trip.

Needless to say Gus didn't have a car like one of theirs. No, it was the station wagon his mother had driven for years, which he'd inherited from his brothers when they moved on to better cars. The back window was knocked out, and you had to tie the doors shut with rope. "Jesus, I hope I got enough gas," he said. "I meant to get some last night."

"Don't worry about it," I said. "If you're going to let me use your board, buying some gas is the least I can do." I had more money than I usually did since my parents had left a reserve for emergencies.

Gus grinned at me. "Well, that's not the reason I wanted you to come along, you know ..."

"Sure," I said. "But every little bit helps, right?"

Gus nodded. "Gotta get a job, my mother says. Make some money to support my bad habits."

He swung the door open, then stepped aside to let me get in. He slammed the door shut and tied it up again before going over to the driver's side, where the door also had to be unhooked and then hooked again. "You can't win them all," he said, pumping the accelerator. "*No se puede ganar todo.* You know what I mean?"

The explosion of surfing came in the middle of thirty years of unusually calm weather in Southern California, from the end of the 1940s to the end of the 1970s. None of the surfers realized it, and it's one of the ironies of life that Gus only discovered it after his accident, when he got serious about meteorology. He told me about it the third or fourth time I came to see him after he was hurt, when he was finally beginning to come out of his depression. It seems, he said, that the water temperature when we were growing up was consistently colder than average, the usual storm track was down the coast from the north. He and I tried, but we could only remember five times in our childhoods when a storm born in the tropics roared across the Pacific or jumped Mexico to thunder up northward, bringing with it high winds and warm rain, instead of cold.

Because of the calm weather, the people who came flooding into California built everywhere: in the dry riverbeds, along the cliffs, close to the beaches. Contractors stripped hills of brush and cut big bites out of them to make flat places for building. Governments piped water for hundreds of miles so people could grow grass and roses. The population seemed almost universally proud at having found this region of wonderful weather and then perfecting it further.

My father, who'd grown up here and seen the San Diego River flood Mission Valley from side to side when he was a boy, knew it was an illusion. Bunch of fools, he said, but nobody listened to him on anything but medical subjects.

Even then, though, some problems had begun to show up. The long stretch of sandy beach that ran from the La Jolla hills south to Point Loma was shrinking, particularly at the southern end. No big problem, said the powers that be. The Army Engineers were right in the middle of dredging the channel into Mission Bay and reinforcing the parallel jetties that guarded the entrance to the channel. The dredging spoils (which were mostly sand after all) had to go someplace, and what better place than the beach? So for months a three-foot diameter pipe spilled sandy water at the edge of the beach, moving seaward slowly as the beach filled in.

The broad, new beach didn't last very long in all its glory. Nobody seemed to realize then that the reason the sand was there in the first place was that it had been washed down from the mountains when the San Diego River was in flood. No floods meant little sand — and if you built dams upstream you'd trap what sand there was behind them.

What is more, in a section of coast where the prevailing currents ran from north to south, an east-west barrier that broke the flow meant sediment would pile up on the north side. Too bad for the beaches on the south. They'd only be replenished when the direction switched. That is, when the big weather systems came up the coast, and that meant not very often in those years.

But the beach was still in pretty good shape the year that Gus taught me how to surf. It was before they built the fishing pier, which has also messed the currents around some; when we pulled into the parking lot beside the lifeguard station, we were a good hundred yards and a breakwater away from where the sand was packed hard by beating waves. I remember that the afternoon sun was shining from the southwest, which meant that we had perhaps two hours of daylight left. Things looked good.

Once we'd parked Gus led me over to the next little street, which dead-ended into the beach. The neighbourhood was first built up between the world wars, as a vacation place. There'd been a trolley line from the centre of San Diego on the other side of the Bay, and when things got tough during the Depression the little houses became homes for carpenters and mechanics and small businessmen. Now there's a Historical Committee or something like that trying to save what's left from those days, and two-room bungalows sell for three times what my parents paid for their big house in a nicer neighbourhood. But this was long before that, and the first six houses Gus and I passed had little front yards covered in patchy grass, or some form of succulent ground cover like pickle weed or ice plant.

My father would have said the seventh one looked worse, because its yard was filled with sawhorses, tools, and wood. No one had driven up the driveway in a while, and it was littered with shavings and dust. The door to the garage at the back of the lot was open. You could hear the whine of a power sander above the distant roar of the surf and the nearer sound of the wind. This was Flynn's place, and Flynn was the best. "Wait 'til you see the board he's making for me," Gus said to me.

Flynn looked up from his sanding when we came through the garage door. He was about twenty-five, wearing cut-off jeans and a T-shirt covered in white powder. He had a handkerchief tied over his mouth and nose, which he slipped down around his neck as he turned off the sander. "Whatcha say, Gus?" he asked, straightening up.

"Brought my friend, here, over to see your works of art. Thought we'd take the new one out."

The guy nodded to me. I nodded back. "You want to take it out?" Flynn said. "Sure, why not? Take it out and see how the fins work now. It's over there in the rack, third from the bottom, I think. I was comparing it with Greco's board."

Along the far end of the garage maybe twenty surfboards rested on an array of supports that stuck out from the wall like waiting arms. Flynn put down his sander and moved toward the rack, while Gus moved to the other end. Quickly they slipped a board out. When Gus had a good grip on it, Flynn let him flip the board up so that it stood beside him, a good foot and a half taller than Gus was.

"Flynn's a genius," Gus said to me, rotating the board so he could see what would be the underside once the board was in the water. "Look what he's done with the fins. With a lighter board, you need a different configuration. Stuff that worked on the old ones doesn't do it."

Flynn picked the sander back up and grinned. "Gotta go with the times, gotta try things out," he said. "Greco thought that maybe if the fins were about a half an inch longer on his, that would compensate for his weight."

"Maybe, maybe," Gus said. But he wasn't listening very closely. He rubbed his hand down the smooth surface. "Feel that," he said to me. "Greatest finish around."

Flynn grinned. "It's new," he said. "That helps." He pulled the handkerchief back up over his nose and mouth and turned on his sander.

"Touch it," Gus said to me above the noise. "Don't you just love the feel of it?"

When I passed my fingertips lightly over the surface, it felt as smooth as ... what? Silk crossed my mind: the silk of the scarves that my mother had worn around her head when she was in chemotherapy to cover her wispy hair. But that wasn't an image that belonged here, so I just grinned at Gus, waiting to see what happened next.

"So what do you say? My other board is over there," Gus said, turning around so he could tuck the new board under his arm. "We'll just get this one out of the mess, get the old one, and get going."

Flynn looked up before we left, but it wasn't a farewell. He was staring out into space as if he could see some perfect board riding some perfect wave, as if he was already going forward in his quest for perfection.

That sounds pretentious and presumptuous, but then Gus and some of the other guys who were normally pretty inarticulate might actually have talked that way. Perfection seemed possible, believe it or not, and the far-seeing gaze was something that you couldn't miss in surfers. They'd be standing around, drinking milk from cartons or beer from bottles, their boards either leaning against the seawall or stuck vertically in the sand. There'd be a conversation going about something, lazy words circling around a subject that had been covered the day before and the day before that: women, varnish, long boards versus short boards, the signs that showed that the wind was going to shift. Then suddenly the words would be left hanging in the air, as something beyond caught their attention. No matter that the sun was glinting off the water, like flames leap from a fire. They stared, pupils dilated despite the glare.

And whatever was happening around them disappeared. It was the kind of concentration you see in hunting animals: a dog at point, the big cat ready to pounce, the boy with the slingshot in the *National Geographic* special about New Guinea. Something important was happening or about to happen, something that must be studied with all the energy available so that the dog or the cat or the boy — or the young man on the beach — could spring into action.

I never got caught up like that. Gus did, he spent hours doing not much, but all the time listening for something, as if he might feel with his feet the smallest difference in the pounding of surf a half mile away. It felt as if there were an invisible link between him and the ocean and its rhythms. I imagine that's part of the rage he felt after the accident: he had been betrayed by the ocean, by forces that until then he had thought were solidly on his side.

I was reluctant to care for much, even Gus in his obsession saw that. After all, there was my mother who'd been so sick. Caring about her mattered, caring about surfing the way Gus did wasn't worth the effort. But I was game to try it that afternoon.

We carried the boards until we were nearly waist deep, then slipped them into the water, pitched forward on them, and began to paddle. Gus headed toward the right of the place where the dredging spoils had been discharged into the water. There the uneven bottom interacted with the row of waves breaking around the jetty to the north, so that there was a line where the tops of the waves curled weakly. It was easier to paddle up the face of the incoming wave, ride over the foam at the top, and continue out to sea on the other side.

By now it was late in the afternoon and the sun stood no more than fifteen degrees above the horizon. I found myself turning my head north so that the light stayed out of my eyes. The water was cold on my arms when I plunged them in to paddle and when the spray from the waves landed on my back. But the air was still warm with the pent-up heat of early fall so the coldness felt almost good.

The paddling was tough work for me, though. Not that I was out of shape really, but by the time I'd joined Gus beyond the breakers I was feeling the effort in my arms.

"Okay?" Gus shouted to me once I'd broken through the last line of waves. Gus already was sitting upright on his board, facing toward the shore, his back to the sun.

"Yeah," I shouted back, as I tried to turn my board around so I could face the same direction. Not a hard thing to do, you'd think, but nevertheless it took me several minutes. While I pulled with one arm and countered with the other, a swell bigger than the ones I'd let pass picked me up. Further north, where the waves were breaking earlier, two guys were already paddling after it, hoping to catch it before it broke. I was distracted for a minute when my left hand snagged on some kelp floating in the gathering wave. By the time I'd freed myself and looked around one of the two was making his move, was up, was riding the wave toward shore.

Gus was face down on his board again, giving a couple of pulls with his arms, trying it out, and then deciding that this wave at this place didn't have it. He let it pass, then shifted so he was kneeling and started to paddle over to me.

"Try it on your belly a couple of times," Gus said. "Do it like it was a paddle board. Get the feel back. Then try to get up."

Another swell was approaching. Gus watched it begin to break at its northern end, then he started paddling. "Come on, try this one," he shouted over his shoulder.

I hesitated an instant, but why not? I pulled with both arms as the board began to move with the roll of the water under it. Another pull, another, then another. It was as if the board were in a current now, moving faster than the strength it showed would warrant. The individual molecules of water rolled toward the shore, pushing the board ahead of them. The rush of gathering forces engulfed me.

Other things give a rush too: downhill skiing, rock climbing, and skydiving all come to mind. But here at the edge of the ocean there is something more. There is a connection with a rhythm begun when water appeared on this world. Stand at the edge of sea or ocean and watch the waves roll in. Then listen to your heart. The beat is the same, you are linked to the planet.

But Gus and I weren't thinking fundamental connections that day. I was just trying to make everything work, and it wasn't easy. I made five trips in to the shore, three on my belly and two on my knees, all only slightly more sophisticated rides than the ones we'd made as kids on air mattresses and paddle boards. But I was pleased with myself.

"Not bad," Gus said. "Now, what you've got to do is practice the moves." The sun had set and we were standing on the beach, shivering as we dried ourselves off on sweatshirts and towels. "Got to get so you can switch from your belly to your knees and then to your feet in about a second."

I nodded.

"What you want to do," Gus was saying, "is get down ..."

"What I want to do is get something to eat," I said. "What do you say ...?"

"Hey, Gus," a girl's voice called.

We both looked quickly toward the street. Annie stood beside a ten-year-old Mercury, the door open, the radio sounding from inside where three other girls sat.

Gus smiled. "What talent do we have tonight?" he said to me. Then, more loudly, "Well, what do you know, it's the nymphs who live by the shore." Then again to me: "Could you loan me a couple of bucks until next week? That way we could get enough for everybody, a couple of jumbo pizzas maybe."

And for once I had enough. For the girls too, which, strictly speaking, I didn't have to do. It wasn't a date, we all were just friends, but I paid.

So I was in a good mood when my parents arrived back late that night. I heard them drive in the garage, because I'd only been in bed about ten minutes myself.

That's strange, I remember thinking. My mother had wanted this weekend so much, the hotel telephone number was posted on the bulletin board in the kitchen, she'd planned everything so carefully. But, selfish kid that I was, I didn't wonder why they had come back sooner than expected. I was simply glad that I was home when they arrived, that there could be no questions in the morning about what I'd done and where I'd been.

But the questions in the morning were about my mother. She was ill again, my father said. I would have to get by on my own for a while.

My first reaction was joy: no one was going to have the time to interfere with my life.

The guilt came afterwards, of course, along with a return of the gloom that had lain over the household during my mother's last illness. This time it was even thicker, because the return of cancer usually means the victory of cancer. But I was right about one thing: my father had no time to worry about me, so the coast was literally clear for more surfing. Over the next weeks — until the water became so frigid that staying out for longer than twenty minutes became impossible in those pre-wetsuit days — I went to the beach often. Not every day like Gus, because I took my school work more or less seriously. But often enough so that I could leap to my feet on the crest of a breaking wave and ride in to the shore, shouting with joy.

Joy. Yes, that's the word. How much joy has there been in my life since? As I sat in my rented Neon by the side of a December-cold ocean, I couldn't say. Joy seemed a universe away. The task I had before me was to consider the incredibly awful thing that I had done that morning and decide what I should do next.

The first of the surfers were arriving, the dog walkers had gone home. It was nine-thirty, and Lil would be wondering where I was. Perhaps the best thing would be to go to the house and pretend that nothing had happened, for a little while at least. I knew I should turn myself in. I *would* turn myself in, I promised myself. But let me get this part of my trip over first. The damage had been done, there had been some dreadful accident and I'd fled. Perhaps three or four hours would pass before anybody figured out who might have done the deed. In the meantime, the least I could do for Lil was make sure she was ready to move.

I started the car engine, I turned on the windshield wipers to clear the mist that had condensed on the glass, I very carefully backed up. Then, as my knee throbbed with the effort of moving my leg and foot to accelerate and brake, I drove down Sunset Cliffs Boulevard, past the new apartment houses and the old churches, the library and the OB Community Center. I crossed Newport and looked down toward the beach and the pier. I saw kids on skateboards, and vans with racks on top for surfboards. I saw an old man out for a stroll with a cane. And then I came to the point where the coast cuts over to meet the road. I turned up the hill at the intersection and then turned right at the second street. Lil was in front, watering the scarlet poinsettias and pyracanthas, one hand on her walker, the other holding the hose.

She let go of the walker to shield her eyes so she could look more carefully when she heard my car. She smiled as I pulled in the driveway. She waved to greet me when I opened the door to get out of the car.

And I braced myself for the pain of my knee, and of everything that would follow.

~

Annie

~

Chuck *came to the hospital to meet* me: Doris had called him as soon as the ambulance left the complex with Will and me. By the time he arrived they'd taken Will into the operating room and were doing something that I didn't even want to think about.

"Perforated lung" is what the medic said, as he tried to cover the hole in Will's chest. The inside of the chest cavity has two layers, which ordinarily lie as close together as pages in a book. But once there's a hole, air comes in from the outside, the lung collapses, and every breath sucks air back and forth through the hole, not through the windpipe, until the person suffocates. You can save somebody with an injury like that, but you have to work quickly and be lucky.

Before the ambulance took off, they got Will hooked up to an IV and tried to stabilize him. He'd lost a lot of blood — he was still losing a lot — and so he was probably drifting in and out of consciousness when the ambulance started down the road to the freeway at sixty miles an hour. I had to hold on to keep from being knocked around in the front seat with the driver, and I prayed that he knew what he was doing. That stretch of road from the complex down to the freeway is a bitch, and in our rehabilitation program we regularly get folks who've smashed up there.

But we made it down okay, and then the driver floored it when he hit the freeway. Inside of ten minutes we were up the off-ramp and in the hospital emergency bay. I was in my scrubs, and I suppose if I'd wanted I could have insisted on accompanying Will into triage. But suddenly I thought I was going to collapse, the seriousness of what was happening caught up with me, and so when they pointed out a place I could sit and someone offered to get me a cup of coffee, I retreated. Then all it took was the sight of Chuck, still unshaved and wearing the clothes he wore to work in gardens, to reduce me to tears.

He sat down next to me and reached for my hands. "Jesus, Babes, you don't need this," he said. "Not my girl."

No, he's not Will's father, but a man never could have had a better example.

After the party at Gus's place, R.J. didn't call Saturday or Sunday. *Just as well*, I told myself. After what had happened with Danny I didn't know how I could look R.J. in the eye. Nevertheless, whenever the phone rang I felt the jolt of adrenaline all the way to the tips of my fingers. But it always was for my brothers or my mother, or it was one of the girls I went to the beach with. Thank goodness it never was Danny.

That week before Easter was beautiful: sunny and warm with just a little bit of fog morning and evening. The water was cold, of course, because the water was usually cold, but that didn't bother my friends and me. We went to the beach three times and lay in the sun, and watched the surfers, and talked about them and school and what we wanted to do after graduation.

Of course I was on the lookout for R.J., but he wasn't surfing with Gus and the others. No, I didn't see him at all until Thursday afternoon. My mother had been at me all week to put in applications for summer work. If I was still serious about going on to San Diego City next year, she said, I shouldn't spend my whole Easter break just lolling around. I needed to get work lined up to pay for my books, I was nearly grown, it was time I acted that way, yadda yadda yadda.

So, in part to get away from my mother's yammering and in part because I knew she was right, I was waiting for a bus to go downtown, wearing my best navy skirt and light blue dyed-to-match sweater set, when R.J. came by in a car his father was driving. He waved, I waved back, and that was all. They didn't stop to offer me a ride. *Nuts*, I said to myself, after he'd passed and I continued to stand in the sun in the clothes, which were too hot for the season. Nuts, nuts, nuts.

I didn't mean anything to him. He'd only walked me home, after all. And after Danny ... after what I had let Danny do to me, how could I expect ...?

No, no. I wasn't going to think about Danny. One of my friends had asked about Danny as we lay on the beach that week, but I had told no more than the story of the way he'd forgotten about me at the garage. That had been enough reason, thank goodness, to dump him. Story over, as far as the girls were concerned, and what they didn't know wouldn't hurt them.

But what I knew did hurt, even though Danny didn't come around, didn't call my brothers. None of them, to my surprise, asked me about him, either. Maybe they knew we'd broken up, maybe they were glad about that. Or maybe it was just simple obliviousness. Whatever, I decided not to wonder about the whys, since that made me think about Danny, and I definitely did not want to think about him.

My mother didn't say anything, but she never asked my brothers about their love lives, either. I was very glad about that, because it would be even worse explaining to her than it would be listening to my brothers' questions.

Nevertheless, as Easter approached I began to think about going to an Easter service. We were members of a church, everybody was then. Ours was sort of Presbyterian, which was the reason my parents picked it — they were Wallaces who'd immigrated from Scotland before the war, and my dad still had an accent although my mother had whittled hers down to not much at all. But the church had also been the first established when this part of Point Loma built up, and it gathered in a lot of middle-class and upper-middle-class families like R.J.'s who bought the new houses. His family didn't go often, but I didn't want to see him there by accident.

The lighthouse at the end of Point Loma was where some civic group sponsored a special non-denominational service, though. Folks called it a sunrise service, but it was held well after the sun rose. My mother and I had been talking about going for several years, but I probably would not have mentioned it had I not wanted to be, what? Forgiven, perhaps? No, not forgiven. What Danny had done hadn't been my fault. But I felt unclean. I wanted, I needed, a spiritual experience, although I would not have put it that way then.

Maybe my mother was wondering about me, maybe she had certain suspicions, because she agreed right away to go to the service even though she'd already said she would pour coffee after the eleven-thirty service at our regular church.

By the time we got near the end of the Point, the sun had been up for a good two hours, but there was still a freshness to the air. A little fog had collected during the night down near the water, but it was gone, and the dew on the sage and other plants was drying. The air smelled good — of the ocean and thick-leafed plants.

I drove, with my mother sitting beside me, fuming a little about the traffic. "We'll have plenty of time," I said as we inched our way up the slope from the Fort Rosecrans cemetery to the lighthouse. The road was only two lanes, and obviously the parking lot would be crowded. "I'll let you off and then go park the car. Afterwards the parking lot will have emptied out by the time we walk back to the car."

I could feel my mother give me a dubious look. One of the things she said was good about having a husband who was an auto mechanic was that she always had a vehicle to take her where she wanted to go. "I saw him with his head under the hood of a car, and I said to myself, 'I'll never have to walk again,'" she would say if anybody got her started talking about when she was young. "He was right good-looking too: what more could a girl want?" Walking in parking lots was sometimes unavoidable, but my mother never did it if she could help it.

"Well, I can't very well go and get the car and come and pick you up at the end, can I?" I said. "That'd take longer than just walking over and leaving from ..."

"Oh, never mind," she said. "I don't know why I agreed to come with you." Which invited a response from me, of course, and which could have led to an argument, but the traffic divided as the road approached the lighthouse so that I was able to squeeze forward into the lane designated for letting folks off.

"I'll save you a seat," my mother said as she got out. I waited an instant to make sure she was all right — a heavy-set woman, moving slowly toward the open area where several hundred folding chairs had been set up. A police officer who was directing traffic began to wave impatiently for me to move on, though, so I swung the car back into the traffic.

Which carried me about half a mile back around the circle toward town. My mother definitely wasn't going to want to walk this far, maybe I would have to come back for her, maybe we wouldn't be able to make it back to our church in time, maybe it wasn't such a good idea to come to this anyway. My head rattled with half-formed worries as I walked along the edge of the road toward the area where the service would be held.

Down in the harbour the sun bounced off the water. Up here, it was still cool. I shivered and wished I'd brought a sweater, even though I had nothing that would look right with the summer dress I was wearing. The women up ahead were wearing suits with jackets: lilac and raspberry and pale grey, the kind of outfit you always saw in department store windows this time of year. I started to skirt around them, moving quickly to warm myself up a bit. My own heels weren't very high, but the back on the right one rubbed a little. Never mind: up where the service would be held we'd be out of the wind, I thought. It would be warmer there and I'd be able to slip off my shoes.

I brushed against someone as I hurried. A small woman, with two men. "Excuse me," I said automatically.

"Annie," a man's voice said. A man? No, it was R.J.

R.J. Suddenly I was not cold, but blazing hot. I stopped and turned around. He was there with his father and mother. She was a small woman, looking thin and pale, being supported by Dr. Mercer on one side and R.J. on the other.

"Hello," I said. There was a quaver in my voice, which I hoped they wouldn't notice. Mrs. Mercer was so frail! But why hadn't they left her off up at the front the way my mother had insisted? Didn't they realize how far they'd have to walk? I wondered if Mrs. Mercer would be able to make it.

A small smile flitted across her face, then fled, as if she could not concentrate on it while she was doing something as hard as walking.

Dr. Mercer nodded curtly. "Introduce us, R.J.," he said. He shifted his grip on his wife's elbow as they continued forward.

"Mother, Dad, this is Annie Wallace," R.J. said, more smoothly than any of the other boys I knew would have. None of them ever made formal introductions, none of them shook hands except before a fight. "Annie, my parents."

But I wanted to be cool, I'd seen folks shake hands in the movies. I tried to straighten my arm out gracefully, but I ended up sort of waving my hand in the air. "How do you do?" I managed to say.

"How do you do?" the doctor repeated, but he didn't seem very interested in me. "How much further must we go?" he asked R.J. "If I had realized ..."

"Shhh," Mrs. Mercer said. She stopped, as if to catch her breath. "This is fine," she said. "I'm doing just fine." But when she took her next step, her legs buckled under her.

"R.J.," his father cried. They both had her, her face looked puzzled as if she was surprised to find that her legs had no strength.

Oh, Lordy, I thought to myself. *They've got themselves a real problem now*. I looked around me, searching for a place where they could sit down. A low stone wall began up ahead, running along the edge of a drop-off. "There," I said. "Bring her up there." I hurried forward and brushed off the rough surface with my hands. Folks hurried past, stepping around the three of them the way a stream flows around a rock. Dr. Mercer's face had turned red, like it had picked up all the colour that had drained from his wife's. R.J. kept his eyes on the pavement, biting his lip, concentrating on keeping his mother upright.

I waited next to the wall, wondering what I should do next, if offering an arm would help or if I should simply disappear and leave them to their own dignity. But I stayed, if only because I wanted to see R.J.'s eyes again, and read in them whatever there was to read.

Once they had her sitting down, Mrs. Mercer seemed to revive a little. Dr. Mercer sat next to her, taking her pulse, letting her lean against him. R.J. stood, merely stood, looking from his mother to me.

His eyes were lovely, ringed in dark eyelashes that contrasted with the grey-green colour. Eyes wasted on a boy, my mother would say. Eyes too pretty for a man, my father might add.

My mother, my mother: I heard the first tentative sounds from the organ. My mother would be wondering where I was.

"Is there anything I can do?" I said. "Do you want some water or something?" I couldn't imagine there was anything, unless it was to go get our car and bring it to pick them up. But that was out of the question. "If not, I probably ought to be going."

R.J. smiled at me. It took an effort for him to do it, I could tell, he had other things on his mind. But he said, "No, no, it'll be all right."

I was pretty sure he didn't think that, so I tried to imagine what actually might help. "Look," I said. "There's bound to be somebody from the Red Cross to do first aid. What if I ran up ahead and found out. We could call an ambulance, see if there are any doctors around ..." I stopped as I realized that R.J.'s father was a doctor, and it seemed there was not much he could do now.

"Yeah, sure," R.J. said nevertheless. "Go ahead. Don't wait for us."

Dr. Mercer didn't even look up.

I found myself running past knots of service-goers, back to the traffic circle where the policeman stood, directing traffic.

I told him breathlessly what the problem was, and waited while he went over to the radio, which crackled on his motorcycle. But the music from the service was starting: a choir blasted over the loudspeaker system, an amplified organ thundered away. My mother would be wondering where I was. "Must go," I told the policeman. "Can't wait."

And sure enough there was my mother, scanning the crowd. I made my way around the great open space where row after row of folding chairs had been set for the service. She'd saved a seat next to her, and the annoyed look on her face suggested that she'd had to fight to save it. I excused my way down the row, getting frowns and mutters as I went. Yes, I knew I was late. Yes, I realized I was disturbing their concentration. But I had a good excuse.

I couldn't explain what it was, though, because the service had begun and everyone was shuffling to their feet to sing "Christ the Lord Is Risen Today." The best I could do was whisper, "Had to help out somebody who was sick," but from the look on my mother's face, it didn't appear she understood.

The sun was still shining, I was out of the wind among all the other worshippers, the music shook the air. But the beauty had gone out of the day. I was not sure I had done the right thing; I wondered if I should have stayed, if Mrs. Mercer was all right, if an ambulance had come for her. If R.J. had been able to help either his father or his mother.

If somehow you could tell what had happened with Danny from the way I looked.

On the way out, when I hurried down to where our car was parked, I searched for a glimpse of R.J. and his parents. My mother refused to walk: "No, I don't care how long it takes, it almost ruined my feet just getting here, and I'm not going to walk any further on the way back. But hurry this time, don't woolgather or whatever you were doing. Surely you can fetch the car in a shorter time than it took you to park it ..."

The words jostled around in my head, bumping against the image of Mrs. Mercer's pale face. But there was no sign of the policeman, an ambulance, the Mercers. So I let the thoughts lie there while I brought my mother back to our own church in time for the last Easter service.

The afternoon was a blur of commands from her in the kitchen, and piles of food on the table, followed by mountains of dishes. My oldest brother's girlfriend helped, but the cleanup took three times as long as it took to eat the Easter dinner. The men, needless to say, were outside talking cars.

There wasn't much talk in the kitchen. My mother always tried to keep a certain distance from my brothers' girlfriends. If she liked a girl, she said, and the brother in question found out, that meant that the girl was out of the picture immediately. If she didn't like a girl ... well, what was the point in talking to her? This girl wasn't a chatterer, thank goodness; there had been cleanup parties where a girl talked on and on, trying to fill up the silence as my mother and I put things away almost without words.

But this girl knew Danny, and the knowledge stuck the back of my mind like a thorn. I didn't want to think about Danny, and since the morning I had thought of him very little. But by the time we'd finished in the kitchen, his presence seemed to emanate from the girl, and I wanted out.

"I'm going to look at the sunset," I told my mother. "I need some fresh air." She looked me over once, quickly, before she nodded.

"Don't wander," she said, finally, the way always she had from the day we moved into the house.

"Sure, sure," I said automatically. Then I fled.

Sunset in actual fact was at least a half-hour distant, but the sun was slanting off the ocean, blinding me as I stepped out the door.

I walked down the driveway, and then crossed Sunset Cliffs Boulevard, to the ocean side of the road. No need to look to see if any cars were coming: earlier in the day there might have been folks out for a Sunday drive, but now the sightseers were gone and the roadway was practically empty. I climbed over the barrier that marked off the top of the cliffs from the road's edge, then began walking slowly south. Down below the tide was out, and a constant stream of some sea birds dove again and again at the tide pools, intent on capturing small fish or other creatures that were now trapped and exposed in the shallow water. I was watching them so intently that I didn't notice R.J. sitting up ahead with his back to one of the posts that held up the barrier.

He saw me first. "I just wanted to say thank you," he said, standing up and dusting off his legs with the flat of his hands.

"What?" I said, not because I didn't hear him, but because I was so surprised I didn't know how to react.

He walked toward me, his hands now clasped in front of him, almost as if he were praying. "This morning, with my mother. You were a big help. Neither my dad nor I knew quite what to do ..."

He stopped just in front of me. We were about fifty yards south of our house. I was aware that if anyone looked out a front window they'd see me.

"Oh, that," I said. "It was nothing." And then, because I really wanted to know. "How is she? Your mother, I mean."

He didn't answer at once, but glanced out to sea. "Not so good," he said finally. "She's back in the hospital ..." His voice fell, and he might have said something more but it was swallowed up in the sound of the breaking waves and the calling birds.

I stretched out my hand and touched his. "I'm so sorry," I said. "Tell me about it."

So we walked down the road, keeping to the top of the cliff, not venturing down its face or out on the rocks. By the time we reached the end of the road, where the hillside that marked the end of the Point began, I had heard a lot, and we were walking hand in hand.

"I'm sorry," he said then, as we stopped at the end of the pavement. "I've taken up all your time."

"No," I said. "Don't be sorry. I was glad to see you there."

He leaned forward then, and gave me a kiss — sweet, at once innocent and seductive.

Afterwards we walked slowly back to my house as the sun slid lower and lower toward the ocean. I don't remember what we talked about: it sort of melted away in the rose and gold light. By the time I stood in my driveway and watched him start back up the hill to his house, what remained was the kiss, and his touch, and the sad-eyed way he told me he needed me.

Which would have been enough, perhaps, but that night I had what I took to be a sign. Some time toward morning I woke up with the moon shining on my face through the window and the centre of my body convulsed in cramps. I lay for a few moments, trying to feel the cold light on my skin. There was nothing, though, only the certainty that something was being expelled from deep inside me. Blood, waves and waves of blood, pushing before them everything that had gathered inside. All pollution. All that had been connected to Danny.

Yes, I told myself, when I was on my feet, finding the pads, washing myself off, stripping the blood-stained sheets from the bed. *Yes, yes, yes*. Perhaps it will be possible, perhaps R.J. and I ...

But then, lying back in the newly clean bed with the moonlight shining on the wall, I fell asleep before I could tell myself just what the possibility might be.

R.J. told me on Monday morning that his mother was in worse shape, and that his father was really upset. "You know things got bad again last fall, but until now we've been hopeful. The last round of chemotherapy seemed to help some. But there doesn't seem to be a lot that can be done now." He paused, and I saw that all the confidence had drained out of him. He wasn't the smart guy, the surfer, the boy who all the girls thought was so cute. He was lost and worried and very sad.

He sighed. "I'm going to see her this evening so I'm afraid I'm not going to have a chance to check the physics assignment," he said. "Could I come by your place on my way home and see if we agree?"

An excuse, of course. If he'd really wanted to check physics, he'd have talked to the other girl on the lab team because she was so much better a student than me. But if he needed an excuse, it didn't matter.

He arrived at our place about nine o'clock: late — my father was already getting ready for bed because he got up before six every morning. I'd been reading in the living room all evening so I could answer the door before anyone else.

"Who's there at this hour?" my mother called. Both of them knew it couldn't be one of my brothers' friends because they all knocked at the door off the garage.

"R.J. Mercer," I called back. "He's come over to get some homework." And then, because I knew my mother would make noises about visitors so late on a school night: "His mother's back in the hospital."

"Oh," my mother said. "Well," there was a hesitation in her voice, but it was obvious R.J. couldn't be turned away under the circumstances, "don't let him stay very long."

"Don't worry," I said, opening the door. But of course I had no intention of shooing him out before he wanted to leave.

First we did what we said we'd do. I had my physics homework spread out on the coffee table, with the blue glass ashtray, which was too good for the family to ever use, moved out of the way. We rarely entered the room: the pale carpet on the floor was my mother's pride, because it was "lovely looking" and because it guaranteed that the room would not be used for ordinary activities. The room looked a little like a furniture store display, which was exactly what my mother intended.

R.J. didn't notice. We sat side by side on the floor, backs to the davenport, with our papers in front of us on the coffee table while he quickly checked things over. Our answers weren't the same, which was no big surprise because he took physics so much more seriously than I did. Homework wasn't the reason for his visit, though, as we both knew.

So when he'd had me change my answers, we sat silently for a few moments. His right hand lay on the floor next to my left hand, the carpet's pile soft under our fingers. The fingers touched, then the hands clasped, and without more words being said, he was in my arms.

Yes, in *my* arms. Quite different from the case with Danny. He'd forced himself on me with his arms, his hands, his wounded pride and pent-up anger. R.J. just leaned against me, slipping down against the front of the davenport so I could hold him against my chest and smooth his hair and kiss his forehead. He was not crying, but I was afraid he might, and that worried me nearly as much as the thought of my father hearing a noise and coming out to see us.

The men I knew then did not cry: not my father, not my brothers after they were older than nine or ten. Danny had snivelled before he raped me, but that was because he was still drunk, out of his head, generally despicable. R.J. was different. I thought that perhaps he'd not yet acquired the usual masculine protective covering, or perhaps his mother's slow slide toward death had worn it away. I did not know which was the case, I only knew that I would do nearly anything for this gentle, sad person.

My oldest brother came in about eleven and stuck his head in the living room. "Oh," he said, as R.J. sat upright quickly. I would be teased later, I knew. My brother would want to know if R.J. was the reason I broke up with Danny, if I thought myself better than the rest of them because I'd taken up with a doctor's son, if ...

R.J. started shuffling the homework papers, making a pile of his, getting ready to stand up. "I didn't realize it was so late," he said.

"Don't worry about it," I said, looking straight at my grinning brother. "You're not bothering anybody."

Nevertheless, he didn't come by the next night, although I dangled a question about what we were reading in English in front of him. He called instead, once he'd got back from the hospital, and this time we had to talk without our physical presence making the connection for us. As I cradled the telephone receiver between my shoulder and neck and tried to retreat as far as possible from the traffic pattern in the family room where the telephone was located, I felt a wave of fear. What could I have to say that would interest him? What had we talked about Easter night?

But the words came, about school, about family, about the future, about poetry. About love, finally.

My mother, however, wasn't so sure. The telephone calls went on too long, visitors during the week in the living room were not welcome, what was I doing about a summer job?

"He's going away next year, isn't he? Does he know what you're going to do?" she asked. And then, softly in my ear, when I was washing dishes and she was drying or when we were sitting by ourselves in the late afternoon watching a soap opera on television: "You know, all I want is for you not to have your feelings hurt."

How could I say that the very last thing I expected was to have my feelings hurt? That I had never, ever felt so alive as I did when I was with R.J.? But to avoid her comments, I pretended I didn't care as much. I said I was going to a movie with the girls and I met R.J. on the cliffs. I invented summer job interviews downtown so I could sit in the car while he went into the hospital to see his mother. I went to church and I walked home with him, the long way around. And then we found our place.

They say that Southern California is where all the loose pieces gather when you take the United States and shake it. I don't know about that — it seems to me that up around San Francisco you get more weirdos — but it's true that you get some nuts here too, and always have. Back at the beginning of the twentieth century there was a group called the Theophosists who loved the climate, and one of them, an

English woman named Katherine Tingley, bought a lot of land on Point Loma. She was a follower of someone called Madame Blavatsky, who Shirley Maclaine played in that movie. *Madame Sousatzka*, I think. Whatever, Madame Tingley built a bunch of Greek-style buildings up on the top of the Point. I've seen pictures from the time, which show a nearly bare hilltop and some domed white buildings. A few of them survived until we were in high school: I remember an octagonal one with windows all the way around that clubs from school sometimes rented for parties. There was an amphitheatre on the ocean side too, which seated a thousand or so: Point Loma High had used it for graduation ceremonies until a few years before, when the graduating classes got too big.

Part of Madame Tingley's estate is Sunset Cliffs Natural Park now, and the rest is Nazarene University. Eucalyptus, live oak, and chaparral cover much of the slopes, which used to be bare, and the surfing is world famous. But the year that R.J. and I found it, there was a chain link fence around the part at the bottom of the hill. That was no real barrier to the few surfers who knew about the beaches, because over the years, folk with wire cutters and shovels had opened holes though it and dug passages under it. When R.J. and I went wandering, we set off along a well-worn track at the end of Sunset Cliffs Boulevard and passed through the fence at any of half a dozen places.

The days were getting longer, which meant that if R.J. went to visit his mother early, we could set off for a walk in the twilight on the pretext of watching the sunset. My mother was not enthusiastic, but I ignored her.

"I tried to talk to my dad about going to Stanford next year," he said the second week we went out walking.

That surprised me. His father had gone to Stanford, he'd always talked about going there when the college prep kids complained about applying to this place and that. "And?" I asked. I couldn't read his face.

"Well, I'm not so sure," he said. There was no smile, his voice was flat, I could not read him either.

He reached over and took my hand. We'd come to the end of the pavement and started down the track that led onto Madame Tingley's property. The sun hovered a finger's width above the horizon, and the weeds we walked past smelled spicy.

"Why?" Actually I could think of several reasons, including one that involved me. But I told myself not to think about it, because that would be asking too much.

And R.J. wasn't ready to explain. He was already saying, "He didn't want to listen to me. He told me not to bother him, that whatever I had to tell him could wait." He stopped walking and grabbed my hands. "My mother's dying, you know. It won't be very much longer."

He looked so sad that the only thing I wanted to do was open my arms and pull him close to me. "There, there," I said, because I could think of no other words to comfort him. His body was hot and damp with sweat.

For a time we stood there, arms around each other. Then a car came down the hill, slowing as it neared the bottom and the turn onto Sunset Cliffs Boulevard. Both of us turned our heads to look at it, and then we simultaneously moved toward the bushes, our arms around each other's shoulders.

Chuck is a landscape gardener, and he'll tell you that this is country where thick vegetation is found naturally only in the cracks in the landscape. He pays attention to that sort of thing, his gardens are so successful because he knows that shade helps plants hoard moisture and that where the summer fog collects and then drips down all night is the best place for greenery. I didn't know that for a long time afterwards. I only knew that night with R.J. that the fog was still far offshore, waiting for the tide to turn. It would come with the change in currents, with the colder water from deep off the coast, riding on the onshore wind. But then the wind was still. In the quiet R.J. and I could have heard the crash of the breakers, if we'd been listening.

We weren't. What I heard was his breath and what I felt was how thin his body was under his shirt. When we came to the first ravine, where the track dipped into the chaparral, I made him stop as soon as we were out of sight of the field and the road beyond. I turned my face up to him and kissed him.

That was the beginning of the first time. There on the ground, in a sandy hollow dug by the winter rains, under scrubby trees. He pushed my shoulders and hips hard against the ground and I would have cried out except that my mouth was filled with his tongue. But I forgave him. His touch electrified me in a way that Danny's never had, and, I must admit, I was relieved he didn't seem to notice that I wasn't a virgin: I never wanted to have to tell him what had happened before.

The stars were out by the time we brushed each other off and walked back to my house. We said good night on the steps. I didn't want to invite him in because I feared that seeing him in surroundings that belonged to my parents and my brothers and my childhood would break the spell.

And it was a spell, a spell that was part sex and part pity, I realized later. But then I wouldn't have called it sex because it was dressed up in the colours of love. My body craved what he could give me, but the mechanics were awkward and love eased the way. How smart of nature to do that. That's what romance is, you know: a way to get young girls to put up with inexperience and insensitivity until they know what they like.

Love is a trap. Romance is a lie. Sex is real, and so is friendship. Those are truths I discovered long afterwards.

The pity I felt for R.J. also coloured what I felt for him. How sad it would be to lose your mother, I thought nearly always when I thought about him. How hard to live with a father as cold and demanding as Dr. Mercer. I would do what women have done forever, I would comfort R.J., I would help him through this bad time. For the moments we were alone together we were the only people in the world. We were the universe, the sun and the moon, the forces of nature.

Mrs. Mercer did not die for another five weeks, and nearly every night until then R.J. came to see me after visiting hours. Most nights we walked to the end of the street and slipped down into the ravine, but once or twice we followed the top of the cliffs and looked down at the waves crashing onto the rocks at their base. Our bodies forced us together with the same strength, despite our good intentions to stop and go no further. Try turning back the tide, try stopping the waves: *I cannot*, I thought, and smiled to myself at the beauty of it.

Then came the morning at the end of May when R.J. did not come to school. I stood on the front steps of the building until the second bell rang, waiting for him. The crowd first boiled around me on its way inside. Then the stream dwindled to a few latecomers, to end with Gus.

He grinned when he saw me. "You're gonna be late," he said. "What will Mrs. Rutherford think of that?"

I shook my head, but I couldn't say anything. I just stared down the steps and across the courtyard, the way that R.J. would ordinarily have come. "I was just waiting for our friend," I said finally. "You haven't seen him, have you?"

And then Gus saw what was happening. "Oh shit," he said. "No, I haven't seen him, and if he's not here I imagine the news is not good." He too looked toward the way R.J. would ordinarily take. Then he glanced quickly over at me. "But it's not going to make anything better for you to be late for class," he said, putting his hand on my elbow. "Come on in, that's what R.J. would want." Then he walked with me to Mrs. Rutherford's class and opened the door for me. I hesitated. From inside came the sound of the class beginning: loose-leaf binders clicking open, papers shuffling, Mrs. Rutherford's low voice telling someone something.

"Go on," Gus said. "Go in, or I'm going to drag you."

Mrs. Rutherford looked up. "Angus," she said. "I thought you weren't due until third period." She stood up from her desk and came over to the door. "Or is this one of your new methods to subvert this institution of learning, coming around like the Pied Piper of Hamelin to lure away the sweet innocents of this class." She spoke with a kind of sharpness that commanded attention, but her eyes sparkled behind harlequin glasses.

"No subversion this morning," Gus said. "Just bringing in a lost sheep."

For just a second, a question flitted across Mrs. Rutherford's face, but then she made a shooing motion with her hand. "Admirable, I'm sure," she said. "You, however, have other commitments at the moment. Get along with you." She allowed me to sit down in my seat without question, and did not call on me even though usually she asked for answers from everyone.

I heard nothing of the discussion, which was about the forms of poetry. I looked straight ahead, aware that various people were reading poems aloud. I'd prepared: if I'd been asked I probably could even have mustered the definition of a sonnet or what constituted iambic pentameter. But even thinking about the subject was too much this morning. R.J. and I had gone over the work together, we'd even read to each other poems about burning the candle at both ends and being young and loving. Poems from a book of sonnets by Edna St.Vincent Millay, which R.J. had found on his mother's bookshelf.

No, that was far too painful to think about.

When the bell rang for classes to change, Mrs. Rutherford tried to stop me. "Are you all right, my dear?" she asked, sounding more conciliatory than I ever remembered. "If you need some help, someone to talk to, I'm here until after four every afternoon."

But there was nothing really to say, and besides, I still hoped I might catch a glimpse of R.J. arriving, so I brushed past the woman without answering.

And so the day passed: waiting, watching, and being disappointed. When school was over I hurried home, hoping that there might be a message, but my mother was gone so there had been no one to answer the phone. For several minutes I stood in the middle of the kitchen and yelled at no one about the unfairness of it all. Then I realized that I was going to have to call R.J.'s house or perhaps even the hospital if I was to find out what had happened.

Girls back then did not call boys. When I told that to my daughters, when they were giggling about calling some boy they were crazy over, they laughed at me. Yes, it was a silly rule, but it was one that even people who had little regard for rules followed. That meant that R.J. had never given me his phone number, so I had to go flipping through the phone book looking for it. The only Dr. Mercer listed wasn't on the street where I knew R.J. lived, but at an address up toward Balboa Park, on what my mother called Pill Hill. I shouldn't have been surprised that the home phone was unlisted — doctors and lawyers often had private numbers — but that meant I'd have to call Dr. Mercer's office.

It took me fifteen minutes before I got up the courage to do it. I sat next to the telephone in the kitchen, rubbing my hands up and down on the tops of my legs, staring out the window toward the ocean. The fog was beginning to come in already: I could see the sun getting ready to descend behind the bank, which lay about a hundred yards offshore. *When I can't see the sun anymore*, I told myself, *that's when I'll call.* And then, when the fog reaches the edge of the cliff. And then, when I count to a hundred.

When I finally did call, the nurse who answered sounded harried. "Who are you? A friend of the doctor's son, you say?" she asked.

"A classmate," I said. I knew I sounded hoarse with the effort of speaking. The fog was outside the house now. The afternoon was over. "R.J. wasn't at school and I was wondering about Mrs. Mercer ..."

"Oh," said the nurse. There was a pause in which she seemed to be weighing the possibilities. "Mrs. Mercer ... you're a friend of R.J.'s, right? ... Mrs. Mercer passed away early this afternoon."

There was a silence at the end of the line as I let the words settle into my mind. "Thank you," I said finally. Then I hung up, gently replacing the receiver on the telephone, as if that would help.

I said nothing about what I knew to my family at dinner. I did my homework, and when nine o'clock came without R.J. appearing I pretended not to hear my mother ask where my walking friend was.

I went to bed about an hour later, and lay there listening to my brothers watching television with our father, to my mother padding around the house and then running water in the bathroom. I even went to sleep.

But then sometime after the house had grown completely quiet I heard the low voice outside my window. "Annie."

For just a second I remembered Danny storming into the house, then standing outside the door to my room, until I opened it and let him in. This was not Danny, I was sure, and I did not want to think about him. I pushed his image from my mind and went over to the window. R.J. was standing there, with his hands in his pockets.

"I know about your mother," I whispered to him. "You must come in."

He sat at my desk, once he'd climbed in the window. I wanted to touch him, but he seemed so closed in upon himself I didn't dare.

"How are you doing?" I asked, sitting down on my bed with my back against the wall, my knees pulled up to my chest so I could hug them.

"Not too good," he said. "I've got a migraine on top of everything else." He looked over at me. I could see that his eyes were red even in the dim light. "And my father wants me to leave as soon as I can."

I had not expected that. "You mean like as soon as exams are over?" I asked. I didn't want him to go away, he couldn't just leave like that.

"I mean like by the first of next week," he said. "He thinks I ought to be excused from the exams, or at least be allowed to take them by correspondence." He moved over to the bed, sitting with his feet planted firmly on the floor, his elbows on his knees. I scooted forward a bit so I could touch his shoulder.

"He thinks I need a change of scenery, that I shouldn't stay around here. He says he doesn't want me to become morbid." R.J. turned his head so he could look at me. "Yeah, morbid. That's the word he used. He wants to send me to one of my aunts until I can go to work at this place in Montana where he's got me a job."

"Morbid," I repeated. I moved so I could put my arm around his shoulder. He was going to leave? I knew I should have expected this, but I didn't want to hear it. "And then you go to Stanford?"

"And then I go to Stanford." He turned so he could meet my arm. He pulled me to him. "But I want to stay," he said softly in my ear. "I want to say goodbye to all the places my mother loved. And I want to be with you."

That was what I wanted to hear, and I know I smiled to myself before I kissed his cheek and smoothed his hair. "I don't know what I would have done without you this last little while," he said.

We talked some more, and I was happy because he was here with me in my room, but I didn't invite anything more, because I didn't want to mix this moment with memories of Danny. And when he didn't push me I took that as proof of his love.

Toward morning, he fell asleep, curled up next to me fully clothed, still clutching my hand. I lay awake a little longer, watching him in the gathering morning light. *He can rest a little longer,* I told myself, *let him sleep. I'll wake him up at six o'clock.* Any later and my father would be moving about, drinking his coffee out in front, listening to his car's engine, thinking about ways to perfect the way it ran. Until then R.J. would be able to slip out the window and head back up the hill to his house. Until then, we'd be safe.

But I went to sleep too. At a quarter past seven my mother thrust open the door: "Didn't you set your alarm?" she shouted. "I suppose you're going to want a ride to school this morning ..."

Then she stopped and screeched. "Oh God, what's happened now?"

Well, at least my father was gone, as were my brothers. If they'd been there, if they'd rushed in to see what their mother was upset about, there is no telling ...

"No, Mother, you don't understand," I began.

"But I do, I do. I understand all too well," she said. She came over and flung back the sheet that covered the two of us. Her eyes flicked quickly up and down our bodies: me, still in my nightgown, R.J. fully clothed. She seemed to be calculating: it could be worse.

"His mother died yesterday," I said. "He needed..."

R.J. sat up, blinking. His cheeks were shaded by a little stubble, his khaki trousers were wrinkled. He looked confused.

"His mother died. Mrs. Mercer died," my mother repeated. She reached out and grabbed the chair that stood next to my work table. "Where is your father?" she asked R.J. "Does he know where you are?"

R.J. shook his head. Then he rubbed his hands across his face before he answered. "He was calling people and drinking whisky when I left," he said. "I imagine he probably hasn't noticed I'm missing yet. He was pretty upset ..."

His voice trailed off as he watched my mother's face. She stood holding the chair, as if it was all that kept her from collapse. "Your poor mother," she said. "Your poor mother."

For a long time, minutes it seemed, all three of us were silent. Then R.J. got up from the bed. "I'm awfully sorry. I didn't mean anything wrong. I just wanted to see Annie because I ..." He glanced quickly down at me. I had pulled the sheet back up around me as soon as he'd stood. Now I looked up at him, trying to send him love and courage.

My mother weighed the situation. She was a practical woman who'd seen a lot so she merely said to me: "Get up, girl, and get a move on. I won't have you late for school." Then to R.J.: "Come along, let Annie get dressed and you go call your father to say where you are. I'll take you home before I let her off at school." She paused and pressed her lips together. "But we won't mention to anyone what happened here last night. Your father would jump to conclusions," she said to me. "And *your* father, young man, has enough to worry about right now."

She made me get in the front passenger seat, even though she looked away when we stopped in front of R.J.'s house. I turned around so I could see R.J., who had the back door open but was staring at the front of his house. Two cars were parked in the driveway, a man's silhouette could be seen through the front window, the outside lights were still on.

"I don't know," R.J. said. Then he looked at me, his face drained of colour as if the blood had suddenly rushed away, leaving him on the edge of life, too.

I reached out and touched his face. He moved forward so he could wrap an arm around my head and shoulders. Neither of us said anything, but then he made a sort of shuddering sound and pulled away from me. "Don't come to the service, I don't want to see you sad. But I'll call you," he said, before he leaned forward again to kiss me lightly on the mouth.

Then he was gone, the car door was slammed shut, and my mother was driving away.

I was nevertheless late for school, because my mother wouldn't let me out of the car until she'd told me just how stupid I'd been to allow R.J. in my room.

Mrs. Rutherford said nothing to me when I showed up fifteen minutes late with a tardy slip from the office. But when class was over she stopped me. "How is R.J.?" she asked. "Angus told me you might know. He stopped in before class to see if you were here."

I stared at her. "You know about his mother?" I asked.

She nodded. "The principal sent around a message. It's too bad ..."

"It is, it truly is," I said. "But if you want to know about R.J., you should ask him." Suddenly I was tired of adults. Suddenly I was simply tired. I took a step toward the door.

Mrs. Rutherford nodded, as if she understood. "I see," she said. She put her hand gently on my shoulder though. I moved my shoulders, to throw off her touch.

She quickly moved her hand away. "Poetry helps," she said. "Write about it." A stupid idea, I thought at first, but then when R.J. didn't call that night, I went walking along the top of the cliffs by myself and some words came to me. I wrote them down when I came home and by morning I had a poem. Before class I put it on Mrs. Rutherford's desk without signing it.

I watched while she read it silently once, twice, three times. "I have a poem here," she said at the end of the class. "The author appears not to want to acknowledge it, but I will read it anyway:

> Our Immortality
> From ages long, long past
> Great thundering masses
> Of green-blue water have crashed
> Against this shore,
> Each retreating wave carrying with it
> Part of the eternal rock

To lands far off —
To lands unborn.

So has it been
Since earth began;
So will it be
When little man has gone his little way.
The coast will change;
New harbours shelter other ships,
New cliffs protect new, wiser nations
From ravages of storm and surf.

And you and I like all mankind, shall fade,
Not see the golden dawn of better days.
And yet our love, like life, remains —
Seen in the calm green depths, the cliffs
Immortal in their change, and best, in the
Sad timelessness of sea and shore's
Tumultuous embrace."

Mrs. Rutherford paused and looked directly at me. "I want the author to know that this is a first-class effort. Persevere, whoever you are."

That, I later decided, was the high point of my educational career, and the reason why I turned to her for a letter of recommendation when I decided to go back to school many years later. But I didn't send the poem to R.J., not even when things began to get more complicated.

He didn't call on Friday, nor on Saturday, which was the day of the funeral service. My mother, who had heard him say that I shouldn't go to it, didn't even suggest going, although she was watching me and the way I didn't stray far from the telephone. On Sunday I waited until she was at church before I called Gus to get the Mercers' home number, but no one answered. So Monday at noon I called Dr. Mercer's office from the phone booth at the grocery store down the street from school.

The nurse answered. "They're gone. Both of them," she said.

I cried then. I cried and cried, and I didn't go back to school. I walked home and then I sat on the cliffs and watched the waves and tried not to think. But that was not the worst.

My mother was the one who suspected first, even before I did. I was busy, I tried to make sure I was busy: the last weeks of school, the last tests, the yearbook signings, the preparations for graduation, the parties.

But on the Thursday morning two days after the end of classes, Danny called. Back long ago, when things had been simpler, I had talked to Danny about going to my senior prom with me. In March, I had paid for two tickets, at the same time that I made the final payment on the yearbook and the class ring that I'd bought, even though Danny had teased me about being so caught up in school stuff. But then when everything began with R.J., I assumed that he and I would go together. I had even told R.J. that the dress my mother was making for me was blue and that I liked white flowers. But he was gone and Danny still thought he would be my date. Now he wanted to know where I wanted to go for dinner before the prom.

"Dinner?" I heard myself asking. I felt awful, I had woken up feeling like I might throw up, and I was certain I did not want to eat with Danny ever. "I don't want to go to dinner. Don't you understand, I don't want to see you."

"You don't want to *be seen* with me, is all," he said.

That too, I almost said, but I didn't because I didn't want to get in a fight with him. Fighting with him would be giving him more importance in my life than I wanted.

What I really said was: "Look, I'm busy, I can't talk now." And then I hung up and went into the bathroom to throw up.

Incident over, case closed, I hoped. Certainly when I felt the nausea roll over me the next morning as I woke up, the thought of eating anything with anybody was repulsive, abhorrent, disgusting.

That's what I told my mother, when she asked what Danny had wanted. "He wasn't around for a while, was he?" she asked as she looked carefully at me.

I was sitting at the kitchen table, my head in my hands. There was a bowl of corn flakes and a glass of milk in front of me, which I'd got for myself, the way I always did in the morning. I poked at the cereal with a spoon, but couldn't bring myself to eat.

"Aren't you feeling well?" my mother asked.

I looked up, surprised that she had changed the subject, because once she had an idea she usually stuck to it. "I feel awful," I said.

"Well, hurry up anyway or you'll be late for church," was all she said.

The next morning she was waiting outside the bathroom door when I finished being sick. "Still not well?" she asked.

"No, worse," I said, heading back to bed. "I don't think I'm going to move today."

She followed me down the hall. Then she paused for a moment as I settled myself in bed. She watched while I reached over to drag the wastepaper basket near the bed and then pulled up the covers. "This is the second or the third day you've felt rotten?" she asked.

"I don't know," I said. "I think I've felt terrible forever." I pulled the sheet over my head, but almost immediately I had to sit up so I could heave into the wastepaper basket. "I don't know what's wrong with me," I said weakly, wiping my mouth on the back of my hand.

My mother watched, and didn't say anything. Outside the morning sounds of the week beginning troubled the quiet. Inside the clock ticked and the curtain blew slightly in the draft from the open window. Finally she asked, "When did you have the curse last?"

I lay back on the pillow. I brought my hands up to cover my eyes. The curse: I hated it when women called it that. "I had my last *period*" — I emphasized the word, I wasn't going to let my mother get away with suggesting that somehow God was judging women — "oh, let's see, back around Easter, I guess."

Blood at the time of a blood sacrifice: now that was a nice idea, I thought. *Wonder how it would go over in a church group discussion, though.* I almost laughed at the thought of the shocked looks the mention of the idea would bring ...

But my mother was saying, "Easter, which was April 22. Today is June 14." She stopped, her face turning red. "Is there something I should know, Annie?"

That was a Saturday. I used to hate Saturday nights, I had my share of Saturday nights with Danny. Saturday nights were what made me leave him.

We were up in Alpine, in the foothills, where we'd moved after Will was born and Danny got a job in a garage there. He was all excited about the move; he was glad to get away from my parents' place, where we'd stayed after we got married until the baby was born. He said he couldn't stand my mother telling him what to do anymore.

So when Danny heard about the job in the mountains he said "yes" right away. And I must admit I kind of liked not having my mother watching everything I did with the baby. We only had a little place in a court that was mostly rented during the summer to vacationers, but it was okay.

It was okay for a while, that is. The first winter wasn't very cold — only a little snow in January, which was kind of fun because I'd never lived where there was snow before, and we all played outside, even the baby until he started to shriek because his hands got cold. And during the spring and summer, there were a couple of other girls with babies in the court. Their husbands were working for the Forest Service, so they were alone a lot of the time, and we would take the kids and drive to a place where a stream ran all year round, and the babies could splash around in the shallows. But at the end of that summer when the nights began to cool off and grow longer and I could see that I was headed for another winter in the court with nobody besides Danny to talk to since the other families had gone back to San Diego, I began to get antsy.

By then Danny had done everything he wanted to the pickup. He wouldn't let me drive it, though. He said that the machine was too good for ordinary street driving.

Which had been both the problem and the attraction of the job in Alpine, I realized later. The little town was supposed to be a great place for racing. Lots of cross-country circuits through the dry countryside. Enough winding roads up and down the mountains. A certain amount of tolerance from the county sheriff's office, because they'd rather see racing on back roads around a dinky little town than in more populated areas.

But at the same time, the pickup was our only vehicle, and when Danny was out in it, I had to push a stroller to the store up a street that had no sidewalks. On the way back with the stroller full of whatever I'd bought, I had to coax a toddler to walk the half-mile home. That got old fast.

I started drinking beer seriously toward the end of that summer, when my Forest Service friends were packing up and heading back to their regular lives. I'd have a beer in the late afternoon after I'd got things squared around and Will was splashing away in a bucket of water behind the house or watching cartoons. I'd sit on the sofa in what we called the living room and read something that I got from the Bookmobile or a magazine I'd lifted from the pile in the laundromat, and I'd slowly sip a beer, making it last.

And then I'd have another beer while I waited for Danny to come home, after I'd put Will to bed. I'd read if I had something interesting, or I'd watch television and stare into space if I didn't. Then I'd sit and drink with him while he ate whatever it was I'd cooked. By the time we went to bed I sometimes forgot to lock the doors and shut the windows. Danny didn't notice, he was usually too far gone to do anything but snore.

Then came the third Saturday in September when Danny was scheduled to race against some guys from Julian and some others who came up from El Cajon. By then he'd won a half-dozen races, he'd developed a reputation, and he was making me mad.

He woke up about 10:00 A.M., which was early for him on the weekend. Will and I were outside already because Will was up before seven, and when he got tired of playing in the kitchen I'd dragged him down to the store to buy beer, milk, and a couple of other things. We'd been back a good half an hour when Danny opened the door that led off the kitchen.

"There's nothing to eat," he said. He'd never played football in high school, but he'd had a football player's build, big and burly. Now, though, he'd begun to put on weight, and his belly bulged under the T-shirt he'd slept in. During the week he usually grabbed coffee and a doughnut at the café across from the garage, but on the weekend he wanted bacon and eggs. Which I had forgotten to get.

"There's cereal in the cupboard," I said. I leaned over Will so I'd look busy with him. "I made some coffee and left the setting on warm."

"Cereal," Danny said, as if it was a curse. "I'd rather drink horse piss."

And it was downhill from there. Instead of horse piss, he started in on the beer, eating a package of tortilla chips and half a jar of Cheez Whiz with it. When I brought Will in for lunch, Danny was stretched out on the couch watching a baseball game on television, even though reception on that channel was so rotten up there in the hills that you couldn't make out the players. He pushed Will away when he toddled over to say hello. The only thing he said to me was, "Can't you get him to shut up?" when Will started banging on his high chair while he waited for me to make him a sandwich.

No, it wasn't until I'd persuaded Will to take a nap, and I'd returned to the living room, that Danny even looked at me. Then, as I got a beer for myself out of the refrigerator and stood in the kitchen doorway, working at the tab on the top of the can, he held out his arm and smiled. "Whatcha got there?" he said.

"A beer," I said, aware that my voice, which I'd intended to be sneering, was wandering toward the nice. I got tired talking to Will. I got fed up with trying to keep him quiet. I was bored with this place. Even talking to Danny was better, and besides, maybe a working man did need bacon and eggs on Saturday morning, maybe I should be sorrier that I'd forgotten to buy them.

"Got one for your big boy?" he said. "He's thirsty too."

I turned back to the kitchen, opened the refrigerator door, and brought out another beer. But as I walked back toward him, I found myself doing a little shimmy, part shiver from the refrigerator's cold, part, I don't know, come on, probably. A last chance to make a connection, maybe?

"Ah yes," Danny said, drawing out the "s" so that it sounded menacingly sexy. "Bring it to your big boy."

The beer we drank afterwards. It tasted good, as did the sweet smoke from the joint that Danny rolled. I fell asleep on the floor once I'd taken three or four tokes. When I woke up, he was asleep himself, with two more beer cans next to him, and what seemed to be a golf match on the TV.

I felt good, for once. I felt like things were possible after all, I felt that things might change. I knew I wanted to race with him that night.

I didn't tell him right away, not that I could have got through to him had I tried right then. He snored all the while I fussed with Will, and he was still asleep when we came back from another trip to the store in the late afternoon. He didn't stir at all until I had Will in his high chair and he was waving a chicken drumstick in the air.

"Smells good," Danny said, stretching. "You barbecue some chicken?"

"Yeah, sure," I said. "From the takeout counter at the market." But it was good. He grabbed the other drumstick from the carcass and then stood nuzzling my neck in between bites. I didn't say anything about his greasy mouth in my hair because I was saving his goodwill for later.

And his good mood continued even after Will and I got in the pickup. It wasn't until we'd driven through the town and to the next one where the assembly point was that he seemed to understand what our being there meant.

"What you going to do while I race?" he asked, as he pulled the handbrake. He let the engine idle, because once it was revved up, he didn't like to bring it down again.

"I'm coming with you." Will was sitting on my lap, drinking milk from a bottle and playing with the edge of the blanket he carried around with him everywhere. The other times Danny had raced, I'd taken him and sat near the finish line with one of the other wives in a Corvette. Will had slept through the races, except for the end when the noise of the winner's honking horn woke him up.

Danny appeared not to hear me at first.

"I'm coming with you," I said again. "We're coming with you."

"What?" he asked, but before I could repeat myself, he reached over in front of me and opened the door on my side. His elbow hit the baby. "No way," he said. "You're getting out. Both of you."

"I'm not," I said. "He's not."

Danny looked at me. He was not a big talker, but then I didn't know many men who were. Up until then our fights had been a hail of words from me hurled at his back as he left, just like my parents' fights. At the end of the summer he had thrown a lawn chair, and a week before he'd kicked a garbage container that was sitting on the driveway. I had got the message then, but I hadn't pushed it. This time, though, he wasn't going to get away with it.

"Things have got to change ..." I began. But before I'd completed the sentence, he had turned, opened the door on his side, and jumped out. Then he quickly pulled all Will's things out of the back of the pickup and threw them on the ground: jacket, blanket, sack with extra bottle and diapers.

"No," I said, jumping out too. I ran around the truck to pick up the stuff up. "He's coming too. *I'm* coming too. And besides ..." I paused. I had been saving this next up, I was only bringing it up because I was so tired of it all. "Besides, perhaps you're forgetting just who paid for this vehicle. You owe me this."

He'd bought the pickup, new of course, with part of the money that my mother had been holding for me. But things had changed. Things had changed with both of us, and he looked at me with eyes filled with a kind of hostility I hadn't seen before.

"Okay," he said. "You win this one." He walked away, leaving me to climb back inside the truck's cab with the kid. I sat, stroking Will's head until he fell asleep. Then I sat and wondered just how cranked up Danny would be when he came back to race.

The plan was: we'd race the circuit, one-on-one, with times kept over the entire course. Once everybody had one chance, the four best times would race a heat one-on-one too, and the two winners would go on to race each other. The circuit would take us up the dirt road that ran behind the municipal dump, then along the fire road that followed the shoulder between the two biggest ridges. Down along the National Forest road after that, past the summer camps, which were silent now that it was September, to the paved county road. This last stretch was the only place that it was easy to pass, the rest of the course was strictly one lane. Which meant that getting around the guy you were up against was tricky at the beginning. The end would be a full-throttle finish.

Once we started I didn't hear the sound of the trucks. It was behind me, somewhere in the dust, trailing after us. I felt myself being pushed back against the seat as Danny accelerated. Suddenly the lights of the starting line disappeared and the dark shadows on the way up the track began to race beside us.

I wrapped my arms tightly around the baby, who had woken up in the excitement of departure, with the yells and the revving engines and the final report of the starting pistol. Will fought my grasp, but I ignored him, holding him all the more tightly. The thought flitted past that maybe I really should have given him to someone else to watch while we raced. But no, this was us together, this was our race. He would remember this ...

I found myself fighting to fill my lungs with air, fighting to keep my heart from pounding too hard, fighting to keep my mouth from ripping open and freeing a long, shrill cry. The kid was crying now, I could feel my breast growing wet with his tears as he tried to bury his face. But that didn't matter, not now, not when Danny was going to race past the other truck, cut in front of him just before we reached the point where the track was only wide enough for one vehicle, where the drop-off on one side would be bone-shattering, and the rocks and shrubs on the other would stop whatever scraped against us.

Oh yes, we were ahead with the other truck on our tail, right on our tail, literally close enough to touch. And Danny was wrestling the wheel to keep our truck out of ruts, to keep it going straight, while he poured on the speed.

And now we had reached the edge of the stretch of road along the ridge, and were plunging down the National Forest road. It was wooded here for part of the way, but the track was wider and the truck behind was trying to manoeuvre Danny over so it could pass.

The kid was screaming, but so was I. Danny seemed not to notice. He flicked his eyes back and forth between the rear-view mirror and the road ahead. Just then the other truck turned on the spotlight that was mounted on its roof, and suddenly our cab was flooded with light, which ricocheted around the dark and then bounced back into Danny's eyes from the mirror.

He swore, a long stream of words that were unintelligible, but had to be curses.

I knew this part of the road from the two summers I'd gone to the summer camp run by the church along this stretch. The pines smelled good here on summer days, and it had been so hot sometimes that the asphalt pavement flowed downhill, forming parallel ridges ...

At least Danny seemed to have control now. At least he had recovered from the blinding light, which still shone through the back window. We'd passed the entrance to the camps, I had seen the signboards flash by, white and stark from the other truck's spotlight. There was a turn up ahead, where the road swung around to avoid the canyon, which plunged down toward the reservoir. The stream at the bottom would be dry now, of course. There never was water in it after April unless there were thunderstorms, and this year there had been none: there would be nothing but rocks in the bottom.

I realized, as the light from behind shifted, that the other driver was trying to manoeuvre himself so he could pass the minute we crossed the bridge over the canyon and the paved road began. Danny saw it too, and hunched his shoulders, shifting his grip on the steering wheel slightly, as if that would help.

Our truck shimmied a little, then drifted a bit to the left as Danny tried to anticipate where the other driver was going. We were almost to the bridge, we would be over in a second, and it wouldn't matter how far the other swung outward to pass because on the other side the road was more than wide enough for two vehicles, there were paved shoulders too, and guard rails along the side that followed the river bed.

Once we were on that stretch all that mattered would be speed, it would be: who could gun it enough to roar down the last half-mile, spin around the bend, and finish first?

"Shit," I heard Danny yell. "Shit, why did I let you talk me into this." He meant having us along, I knew, my weight and that of the kid would be enough to make the difference. "Gotta do it, gotta do it," he shouted.

And then I felt him brake just short of the bridge, just where the road was closest to the canyon, just where it would be worst to go out of control.

"You fool," I was shouting. Will was hysterical now, but I still held him tightly to me. I braced myself. I expected the impact to force my arms open. I leaned forward to protect him.

But the other truck didn't hit us. The driver must have lost his nerve, swerved to avoid hitting us and gone into a desperate skid, because suddenly the bright light was gone. Suddenly the race was over, and there was no question about who won because we were the only vehicle left. The noise of the other truck crashing echoed behind us.

Once Danny had got control back — because the rear of our truck swung around too — he sent us straight down the paved road as fast as we could go. Then, when he arrived, he reached across and opened the door for me. "Get out," he said. "You've had your fun."

The others had heard the crash, and two guys were already in their trucks. But by the time we got to the bridge the other truck had exploded and there wasn't much left except a flaming heap of metal on the rocky bed of the dry stream.

Somebody along the way — one of the old folks who lived year-round now in a summer cabin — had called the sheriff, and Danny was arrested once the deputies arrived. He thought it was funny, he laughed that it was good to be recognized by the authorities for his outstanding driving. And everything would have been forgotten two days later, except by the folks immediately concerned, because the sheriff had other fish to fry. It had just been a back road accident, people had been driving too fast, what a terrible shame. There was an election coming, though, so there was an inquest. For more than a week the papers were full of the wreck, and lawless young people making death traps of our peaceful country roads.

I was right there next to Danny in the courthouse when he was called to testify, but I hadn't figured on R.J.'s father being the medical expert. He usually didn't do stuff like that, he was a surgeon attached to the university hospital, he rarely got involved in accidents. But they were short-handed. Vacations, the usual experts sick, or something. And this was such a hot issue that the inquest had to go ahead, fast. So he'd been enlisted, doing a favour for his doctor friends, or his political allies.

Or was it that? I never knew. I only listened to his testimony about the cause of death. The other driver was killed on impact, his body thrown clear of the truck. The burns on the body followed death, occurring when the underbrush was ignited by the explosion.

All very straightforward, nothing that Danny could be charged for, except speeding.

But R.J.'s father watched me while he testified. He kept his eyes on me afterwards when the coroner prepared to recess the inquest. He waited until I got up and was walking out with Danny, he stood at the door to watch me leave. He didn't say a thing. He followed us into the elevator in the courthouse, I could feel him standing behind me. Still he didn't say anything, he was just there.

Finally, when the elevator doors opened at the first floor, I turned around to look him straight in the face. "I'm a good mother," I said.

He didn't look surprised, although the men with him did. He merely nodded, and without smiling, without saying a thing, he walked down the hall and away from me.

"I'm a good mother," I repeated. But he didn't hear. Nor did Danny, who was up ahead, already barging through the courthouse door.

And that was the end. I knew I couldn't be a good mother and stay with Danny.

There was some money left, my mother still had it in the bank. I decided use it to go to City College and get trained in something that could support us on our own, so we wouldn't have to depend on anybody, so we'd be free.

Will and me. Me and Will.

Chuck didn't come into the picture until the summer that Will was five, and I'd just started working full-time. While I went to school, Will and I lived with my parents — no other way to do it, although it had been difficult to move back. But once I had a job we moved out, and Will was in daycare until school began in September, and for once my life seemed more or less under control, even though Will was still in a cast because of the reconstructive surgery on his leg.

The day that Chuck offered to help had been one of the worst in a couple of weeks. First of all, I'd had to work a 6:00 A.M. to 3:00 P.M. shift, which meant that I'd had to deliver Will to the babysitter's house before they were really up. Will hated that. He didn't like me working at all, but that was another story. I had no choice.

Arriving at the babysitter's so early, though, meant that Will was plunked down in front of the television to watch whatever was on. Once down on the floor he couldn't get up without help because of his cast. The two other boys who also arrived early were a little younger than him, and weren't any more pleased than he was to get up early. They also were bored by the news and cartoons mix on TV at that hour, so they livened things up a bit by taking turns "borrowing" his crutches or the lunch box he brought a snack and his little cars in. They'd do it very quietly too, so as not to disturb the babysitter's own children, who she wanted to sleep until she'd had a chance to shower and get her husband off to work. "Shh," they'd say, when Will protested, "you don't want to wake everybody up. You know what will happen then."

And that would work for a while, but finally the disappearance of Will's favourite car, or the kidnapping of his new GI Joe, was more than he could take. Then he would shout, and without fail, the babysitter, who probably by that point was dressed and almost ready to begin her day, would charge from her bedroom, hairbrush in hand, and flail around her. She did not hit anyone hard, that would have been the end of her career as a babysitter, but the other boys would laugh, and Will, because he couldn't move, would be the one who got it. Just a tap really, didn't even hurt, but it was the unfairness of it — when he had done nothing at all — that made him hate the place.

I suspected this, but I did not ask any questions. Maybe I should have, because it could have been a lot worse, real child abuse. But I needed a babysitter badly, I had to keep this job. I hoped that whatever Will was going through was nothing more than normal.

But that day Will obviously had been on the losing end, and he wanted to tell me about the fights he'd had. I brushed him off because I had no time to even begin to deal with the problem. He had another follow-up appointment with the pediatric orthopaedic surgeon, the last one he gave that day. Nevertheless we had to rush to get there on time.

The news was about what I'd expected: the x-rays showed the leg healing well despite the multiple fractures and the complicated piecing together the surgeon had had to do. But the doctor was running behind, and I'd had to use the stroller to get Will from the car into the medical building and upstairs to the doctor's office. He hated that, he was embarrassed at being wheeled like a little kid, and by the time we were done, he was tired, hungry, and cranky, and so was I.

The stroller was not one of the new ones, which folded up to be no bigger than an umbrella, but one my mother had found at a garage sale, the big and sturdy kind. It was supposed to collapse, but the mechanism was a bitch to work. Up in the mountains when we were there with Danny, it didn't make a difference, but since I and Will had moved to town, it had been sitting in the corner of his room, forgotten under piles of clothes that wouldn't fit in the closets we had. I forgot it was there, even, or I would have got rid of it, sold it or put it out for the trash, because who needs a stroller when your kid is almost ready for school?

No one, unless the kid gets hurt and can't walk for a while. Then you fill the space where a little kid would sit with a couple of cushions so the big kid can sit on top with the leg in the cast stuck straight out in front. If I'd been a sunny soul I might have said that the stroller was a sort of silver lining to the cloud. But I knew it wasn't: it was only a way to get poor Will around when the distances to travel were more than he could do on his own on crutches.

"Yes, yes, I promise, we'll get rid of it as soon as you can walk, and we'll never get one again," I was telling him, as I tried to get him properly settled in the car. It was after six-thirty, and the next step had to be driving through the Jack in the Box or McDonald's. To wait any longer before eating meant disaster. In fact, I was wondering if there was a vending machine somewhere close by where I could get candy bars for both of us to tide us over.

Chuck wasn't in uniform, but I was sure from looking at him that he was military. His haircut was neat, and his moustache was well trimmed. He was wearing well-pressed chinos. Nobody but an off-duty enlisted man would look simultaneously as neat and as casual early in the evening of a weekday.

I was immediately on my guard. Growing up in a military town you get a little wary of servicemen.

"Would you like some help, ma'am?" he asked, stepping forward to grab the handle of the stroller. His voice was slow, and he had a drawl that came from some border state. Before I could say anything he had found the latch that was supposed to allow the handle to be folded into the frame. He shook it, then reached in his pocket for something.

I was about ready to answer that no help was needed when he pressed something, jiggled something else, and the stroller folded down.

"Got left out in the rain, huh?" he said, giving me a smile. "You want this in the back seat or the trunk?"

"The back seat," I said, surprised that he'd been able to fold it up so easily.

He already had the door open and was turning the thing on its side so he could fit it in sideways in front of the seat.

Will was twisting around to see.

"This your engine, sport?" he asked.

"No," Will said. "It's a little kid's thing. I'm just using it until I get my leg working right. See, I got a cast."

He leaned forward over the back of the front seat so he could see Will's leg. "Yes, indeed. One of the walking wounded, huh?"

Will giggled. "Walking wounded? If I could walk, we wouldn't need the stroller. But I'm going to be all right real soon."

"Sure thing," he said. "Don't have a doubt in the world as to that." Then he straightened up and backed out of the car. His smile beamed back at me. "That's the spirit," he said.

There are times when you do things that afterwards take your breath away. Sometimes the motivation is quite clear: I had no clear memory of running to Will when he was hurt that time, but the reason was obvious — I had to get to him. But sometimes even in retrospect the reason is lost. This was one of them. "I don't know how to begin to thank you," I said. "Maybe Will and I could buy you a hamburger?"

Classic, right? Only in the movies it's the other way around: the boy asks the girl. Well, he wasn't a girl, and neither was I, anymore.

I used to tell the kids that I was lucky in love, no matter that I had a couple of false starts. When I found Chuck and he found me, the stars were shining on us. Sounds corny, but it's true. That's one of the things about songs and poetry, you know: they say things that are true and that ordinary folks can't find the words for.

He was a straight-arrow guy, I could see from the beginning. He wasn't going to mess around with me. He was too old, and he'd seen too much. He'd done two tours in Vietnam, and to this day there are parts of that experience he's never spoken about to me or anyone else. I also know that he'd been badly hurt at least once by a woman. He was married when he shipped out, but it didn't last the length of his first tour over there. He offered to tell me everything about it — she'd fallen in love with one of his old friends, he said — when I told him he should know about Will and his father.

"You were married before, you have a son, your former husband lit out for the territory: what more do I need to know?" he said.

"But don't you want to know what happened?" I said, because I really wanted to start this relationship off right.

"No," he said. "There are a few financial and health things you should know. I owe $3,250 still on my car, my father died of a heart attack at fifty-three, and my mother developed diabetes two years ago. But unless you've got debts bigger than that or some dreaded disease in the family, I don't need to know any more. I like your boy, and I love you, and that's what matters."

So of course I didn't push him about his past. And I didn't tell him the truth about Will.

~

Rick

~

M*y father and Lil met when she* was campaigning to make a park out of Sunset Cliffs and he was furious that some developer might spoil his view of the ocean. Or that's what he said. She says they must have met my last year in high school because someone came to parent-teacher meetings about me. She still had the grading sheets from that time, she had nearly forty years of papers for the thousands of kids she taught.

Of course my mother was not in any shape most of that year to do the things that mothers, not fathers, did back then. Fathers went only when there was no other option, unlike now, when I volunteer one morning every two weeks to give cooking lessons to Cassis and her class, when both Jenny and I attend every meeting and every program. Even with the boys I was there a lot of the time. Ask them, they'll tell you about the afternoons I went with them to pick up their report cards and trek around from teacher to teacher to hear why they did so well or so poorly.

Bad days, those. We were in Montreal, and Caroline insisted the boys go to French schools, but she always taught afternoons and she would never postpone any of her classes. So I, even though I could not speak more than a dozen words in French, had to be the visiting parent since the two places where I worked during those years both had good family obligation plans even back then. A few of the teachers spoke English well enough to talk to me so I could understand, but most of the time I had to rely on the boys to translate. They lied to me, I'm certain. I could never prove it, but I would come home after those exercises furious with them but not able to say just where I'd been betrayed.

There's an irony in that, of course, because I owe my freedom to that trip Jenny and I took to France. The little French I did learn helped me there, as did Lil's suggestions of where to go.

That was later. Lil didn't agree to marry my father until after she'd put her teaching days behind her and had finally retired. He'd been after her for years, although he had said nothing to me about it. I imagine he was still feeling a little chagrined about the marriage he jumped into after my mother died.

That had been a surprise too. I came home for the first time in five years to discover a box of tampons in the bathroom I usually used. They were just sitting there on the counter next to the sink, placed as casually as the toothbrush that I left at Caroline's during that period. A sign of someone who was comfortable in someone else's place, who spent a lot of time there, who belonged.

When I saw them, I didn't know what to say. I don't think I ever saw a tampon or a sanitary napkin during my mother's lifetime, although she had told me about menstruation in the little birds and bees talk she gave me when I was ten or eleven. I didn't remember much of it, things were sort of muddled together, and I had the impression that women's periods began when they were married. In fact, the first time I heard of a girl my own age having one I was shocked. Not that I let on about my ignorance, because the person talking was one of the guys at boarding school, who'd snuck out to meet one of the town girls.

"The red flag was up so she sucked me off," he said, as we guys stood in the bathroom, brushing teeth, washing faces, and (those of us with some facial hair) shaving. He was a skinny guy with pimples, who got caught off campus three months later on a Friday night with a mickey of rum in his pocket, and only came back long enough to collect his clothes.

But then six sets of eyes stared at him in the mirror above the sinks. Nobody said anything for a moment as razors scraped around mouths and toothbrushes worked up and down. I don't think the others were as ill-informed about the age of the menarche as I was, but certainly they all were surprised — and maybe shocked — to hear what turn the guy's adventure had taken.

"Red flag? You mean she had the curse? How could you touch her?" my roommate finally asked, rinsing off his razor in the sink. The way he shook off the suds and whiskers indicated just how disgusting he thought the whole thing was. "Girls with their periods are unclean," he said.

"Yeah, my dad says they secrete a kind of poison," the guy next to me said.

That didn't sound right — I couldn't imagine women doing anything as unpleasant as becoming poisonous — but I realized it was something I should look up in one of my father's medical books the next time I went home. I should check out when girls start menstruating too, and I kicked myself for not doing a little more research the last time I'd been back.

But all I said was, "Gross."

By the time my father took up with Mrs. Bellamy, though, I knew a great deal about women because Caroline had explained everything to me that she thought I ought to know. We were getting married in August, and because she wanted to see where I'd grown up, I'd gone back to San Diego instead of meeting my father someplace like my aunt's ranch on the

Russian River or my grandmother's place in Montana as I had every holiday since my mother died.

Caroline arrived a week after I did, a week when I wondered if I should say something about the tampons and then decided not to when my father announced he had someone he wanted me to meet.

"Mrs. Bellamy works for my accountant," he said. "She is a very intelligent woman who has been extremely kind to me lately. When your fiancée gets here I would like to take you all out to dinner so you can get acquainted." It was a speech given as if he had rehearsed it, and delivered as he was going out the door, headed for his morning rounds at the hospital. He knew I was barely awake at that hour and would not comment or question then. By the time he came back home I had decided to let it ride, to wait to see what this woman was like.

She was good-looking, I'll say that for her. Tall, blonde, and tanned, wearing an emerald green pants outfit made of some material that looked soft to the touch, and dangly crystal earrings, plus a ring with a large green stone on her left index finger. Nothing like my mother, but that was okay, I think I would have been angrier if she'd been an artist or from an old San Diego family or any of the things that my mother had been.

Caroline was convinced from the first that she was after my father's money. "Did you take a look at that ring? That's not glass, that's a real emerald, I bet, and I also bet that your father gave it to her."

I must have looked surprised. We were sitting in the darkened living room after the dinner with my father and Mrs. Bellamy, and now my father had gone to take her home. He'd quite pointedly put Caroline in the guest room, while I had my old room, and I'd been thinking that we'd be stupid not simply to go to bed in Caroline's room while he was away.

"He probably needs the sex too, he must not have had much those years your mother was ill, and she's been dead quite a while now," Caroline went on while I tried to digest the idea that Mrs. Bellamy had ulterior motives in taking up with my father.

Sex and parents: always a delicate subject, and then I simply didn't want to think about it. It took Jenny to get me over that. The sex that interested me then was what I was planning to do with Caroline and her soft, big breasts, her smooth skin, her welcoming arms. This was the time when she believed that sexual enjoyment was essential for an individual's optimal development. That meant she worked hard at doing what I liked in bed, as long as I did to her the things that pleased her. Not a bad trade-off. Too bad, in a way, that it didn't last.

Nevertheless, I felt I couldn't just let her reduce my father to a sexual animal. "Oh come on," I said. "She's not a dummy if she's an accountant."

"She not an accountant, silly," Caroline said. "She's a bookkeeper, and she's very well placed to see exactly how much your dad has. She knows what she's getting into. Your dad doesn't. He's being led around by his dick."

I had been sitting with my arm around her shoulders, but we had not progressed to anything more than a few open-mouthed kisses. Caroline reached over and began to wiggle her hands into my pants pockets. "By his dick, " she said. "Like you," she added when it became clear that I couldn't not respond to her.

Caroline, Caroline: we were married for nearly twenty years and had two boys together, and many, many arguments. She left me by the side of the road, so to speak. She's written three best-selling books about modern education and she teaches at both

McGill and the Harvard School of Education. When Cassis was ready to start school, she sent Jenny — not me — a list of the best day schools on both sides of the Hudson with a note that said she thought any child of mine needed as much help as she could get.

But she was right about Mrs. Bellamy. The ring indeed was an emerald, and the earrings weren't crystal but diamonds. In the eighteen months she and my father were married, Mrs. Bellamy completely shook up his holdings, getting him out of safe stuff like PG&E, the utility company, and into Xerox and Canon, which were doing reasonably well, but which were riskier. He was furious at what she'd done: no woman could go behind his back and remake his portfolio, what was all this about getting out of conservative investments, just how much had she gotten out of it all? Then he was even angrier when she wanted a big settlement because his net worth had actually gone up from the investments she had made for him. I never asked what he finally gave her, although he told me much later, once when he'd been drinking all day, that he would have paid anything to get rid of a woman who was as "vulgar and unfeminine" as she was.

"Vulgar and unfeminine," those were his words. Caroline laughed when I told her.

"What does that say about their sex life?" she said

It was at a point when ours wasn't going very well, and I didn't answer.

After that I don't think there was a woman in my father's life for nearly ten years. I wasn't paying much attention. My life wasn't unfolding as I'd hoped.

I took English from Lil that year I went to Point Loma. She also was a guidance counsellor, but I didn't have any contact with her in that regard, I guess because I came in at the end of high school and because I had been slated to go to Stanford from the time I was little. The requisite number of science, foreign language, and math courses had been programmed into my genes, sort of. There was no question that I'd be completely qualified, and in those days when admission standards weren't quite as crazy as they are now, there was no doubt that I'd get in.

Lil understood that, she was from the same kind of family as my mother's. Actually they knew each other. Lil was a little younger, but they had both been members of ZLAC, a rowing club.

San Diego had debutantes and balls and all that, but according to my mother, the girls from the nicest families with the oldest money were more likely to row than to worry about being presented to society. "This is not Boston or New York, not even San Francisco," I remember her saying when I was thirteen. The daughter of a doctor who shared my father's office building made the front page of the women's section in the newspaper just before some debutante ball, the Harvest Ball or the La Jolla Ball, I don't remember which. "Who do they think they're fooling?" she said when she saw the picture.

The girl was very pretty, as I remember, and I'd had a crush on her since I was nine and our fathers' offices had been opened with a cocktail party. I remember following her around that afternoon, watching her from corners, thinking I'd never seen such a lovely thing. She was five years older and we met only three times, but she was one of the girls who came to me in my dreams as I grew older. And there she was in the newspaper, looking gorgeous in her white strapless dress with the crown of flowers on her head, and her father standing behind her. I would have been very pleased to be old enough to go to the dance and take her in my arms and waltz her around in her pretty dress and look down her lovely cleavage.

My mother laughed at me when she saw me with the newspaper spread out on the kitchen table, staring at the girl's picture. "You can do better than that," she said. Harsh words coming from her, which is probably why I remember them.

But the rowing club went back to the end of the nineteenth century, and was both more exclusive — only forty-five girls could be members at any time — and more interesting than any group of girls who called themselves debutantes. It was still going when I was in high school, and a few girls from Point Loma belonged, although I don't remember them being very classy. Be that as it may, Lil and my mother belonged, and Lil remembered her well.

"Tell your mother hello for me," she said the second week of class, when she'd made the connection between us. "Tell her I took up single sculls a few years ago."

I nodded, a little surprised at the attention from her. Mrs. Rutherford was legendary, I'd heard about her the last time I'd been in public school in San Diego because her reputation had filtered down to the junior highs. She was nearly six feet tall, with hair cut short so that it curled all over her head. I think at one time it was called a poodle cut, but I'm certain she had it before the style was named, and she wore it long after the name was forgotten. Hairstyles were something she'd brush away with her hand, the way she dismissed objections or excuses or silliness on the part of students.

She did wear makeup, though: a mouth outlined in a darker colour than her lips were painted, eyebrows tweezed to a narrow line and then filled in with dark pencil, and false eyelashes. I used to stare at her in English class and watch her eyebrows go up and down and her big hoop earrings swing back and forth when she read poetry. She reminded me of someone, but it wasn't until I came across a photograph of Bette Davis playing Queen Elizabeth I that I realized who.

Her accent was different from what we heard around us, too, and the girl who made the fourth in our physics lab thought she sounded English. How a San Diego girl could acquire an English accent was unclear, but we all knew that she'd spent a lot of time in Europe. Mr. Rutherford — Captain Rutherford, my mother said — was English. She'd met him when she went abroad between her junior and senior years at Mills College. The year was 1939 — not a very good one to travel — and the rumour was he was in the RAF and was killed over France. I asked my mother about that, and about the story that Mrs. Rutherford had been a member of the French underground, hiding out in the south of France and lighting signal fires to guide air strikes and naval operations. But by then my mother had begun to forget anything beyond the circle that included me, my father, and her pain.

At first when my father began to write about Lil, I had no idea there was a connection. Then he called to say that he was going to marry again, and Lil came on the phone, and I'd have recognized her voice anywhere. The pieces fell into place, and I began to think how small the world was.

My father said he hoped that Caroline, the boys, and I would come out that summer for the ceremony, and Lil even wrote a letter, saying how good it would be to see me and my family. I didn't want to go, though. I'd quit the bank two years before because I couldn't stand another day of figuring growth strategy, and I'd gone to work for a big investment trust. I wouldn't stay there long, as it turned out, but I didn't want to listen to my father ruminate over how much better off I would be if I had continued pre-med and not switched to economics.

The MBA didn't impress him at all, and I was certain he would snipe at me for as long we were in San Diego about what I might have done, and what sons of friends had done. Nor did I like the idea of Lil sitting there, comparing me with all the other graduates of Point Loma High School she'd taught.

Caroline wanted to go, though. I see now that a trip to the West Coast fit in nicely with her plan for getting her message out, but she talked about what a good time it would be to travel with the boys. Before they'd been impossible, and later they'd be insufferable, but now Richie was eleven and Matt was nine, and they ought to see their grandfather and meet his wife, she said.

So I agreed. It helped that Caroline was enthusiastic about my job change. She thought I was finally getting someplace, she talked about me maximizing my potential, she said it was nice that I was going to be paid more and we wouldn't have to worry about the money for the boys' tuitions.

She talked the job up to my father on the phone and in letters, too, and he was sufficiently persuaded that I wasn't completely wasting my life that he asked how it was going as soon as we got off the plane. Lil was there to greet us at the airport with him, too.

"This is my son," he told her, taking me by the elbow and leading me over to her. "He's put on a little weight, you probably wouldn't recognize him if I weren't here to tell you who he was."

I shook her hand, smiling, pushing Caroline forward, grabbing Matt before he climbed on the luggage carrousel from sheer joy at being liberated from the plane.

"R.J.," Lil said to me, smiling back. "James, I'd recognize that intelligent face anywhere," she said to my father.

R.J. That stopped me. Nobody but Gus had called me that since I went to Stanford. Perhaps my biggest act of rebellion at that point was deciding to claim a real name for myself. My birth certificate read Richard James Mercer III, but just as my father was Dr. R. James Mercer to avoid confusion with his father, Dr. Richard J. Mercer, I'd always been called by my initials at home and school.

"I'm Rick now," I said. "Although your husband thinks it sounds like I'm an actor trying to be someone who has a saloon in Casablanca."

Her hair was still short and curly but had gone completely white. Her shoulders had begun to curve forward with arthritis, so she didn't stand as tall. But her eyebrows still arched upwards and gold hoops swung from her earlobes, grown long themselves with the weight of decades of heavy earrings.

She laughed. "In that case, you'd be calling yourself Humphrey, though," she said. She turned to look at my father. "James, I much prefer Rick."

He was smiling in a way I hadn't seen in years, and even though he was more stooped than he'd been the last time I'd seen him, he was tanned. *She must be insisting that he get outside more, they must be walking along the cliffs or something like that,* I thought.

He put his arm around her. "A woman of definite opinions," he said. "I told you that she beat back the developers practically single-handedly to make the park. The city was going to sell off the land for hotel developments. She got petitions organized and she had people set up a public relations campaign and ..."

"Yes, of course," Caroline broke in, because she could never allow the conversation to drift far away from what she did and what she knew. "Lillian Rutherford, teacher with the terrific technique: there was an article in *Teacher and Community Action.*"

"Teacher? She's a teacher?" Matt said. "She's too old to be a teacher." Then he ran away from me before I could grab him.

Nevertheless, that wasn't a bad trip, and Caroline and I didn't fight very much. It was also the first time that we'd stayed long enough for the boys to get a chance to climb on the cliffs and poke around in the tide pools. Once the wedding was out of the way — a civil ceremony followed by a dinner out in a restaurant on the Bay — we did a lot of tourist things: the zoo, the wildlife park, SeaWorld. The best times were on the beach, though: we rented boogie boards and I took the boys out in the waves. Caroline sat on the dry sand wrapped up in a caftan and read stuff for her dissertation, but even she seemed more relaxed by the end of the second week.

I took the boys with me when I went to see Gus. Caroline let us off where he was staying and then she headed for the school district offices. She was pretty excited, as I remember: she was scheduled to talk to a bunch of reading teachers, convened especially to listen to her. It was the first sign that her reputation was growing.

Before she drove off, she warned the boys again: "Don't stare at this man. He'll look a little strange, but remember that he's the guy who invented that game you like so much."

So they were prepared for him, but I never was when I went to see him. By then he'd been paralyzed for more than fifteen years, and I'd visited him three or four times at various points in his recovery. To see him sitting there in his motorized wheelchair, with his head propped up and his hands and arms arranged so the little movement they were capable of could be translated into commands for the chair and his gadgets — well, in earlier days I would chug a six-pack after seeing him, just to get my balance back.

This time, though, things seemed better than they had been. Caroline was right: his work, if not his name, was famous with kids. The royalties from his games allowed him to get whatever new equipment came on the market, and he'd just bought into the rehabilitation place where he was living. It was brand new, just opened, looking naked as it sat on the still un-landscaped building site.

The inside was finished, though. "How do you like it?" Gus asked me when the aide showed us up to his apartment on the second floor. He had two big rooms. One was a bedroom and living room combination with a hospital bed and a lift to get him in and out of it, television, sound system, panoramic view of the eastern mountains, plants, pictures on the wall, big chairs for visitors, all the comforts of home. The other room also had a view of the mountains, but the curtains were half pulled, and computer stuff covered every surface. "I had a decorator come in and choose the colours and all that, but she just walked out when I started talking about what I needed for my work area."

The boys made a beeline to the three Macintoshes, which Gus had on a long work table set against the wall.

"Hey, Dad, look at this," Richie said. The Macs had only been on the market a few years, and neither of the boys had had a chance yet to play with one. All three screens were filled with little figures of a miner looking for gold or something. "Cool."

"Can we play?" Matt asked.

I was just about to say no — the boys could do a lot of damage — but Gus was wheeling over to the machines. "Sure," he said. "You're just what I need right now. Guinea pigs."

"We really can't stay," I began. "Caroline is coming to pick us up in a little while. We don't want to get you tired."

"Tired," Gus said, and laughed. "Hey, don't worry about me." The boys were pulling out the chairs in front of the work table. "That's right, sit down and reboot with this floppy," he said to them.

Then when they were set up, handling the mouse like they'd been doing it for months, he grinned up at me. "So what're you doing these days? What brings you out here?"

"My father remarried, and we came out for the wedding. Actually my new stepmother told me that you'd moved here."

"Your new stepmother?" His eyes lit up, and I began to suspect that gossip probably gave him a lot of pleasure. "I heard your dad married some flashy blonde about the time you married Caroline but that it didn't last. And you say he married again? Who this time, another looker?"

Yes, of course, there must have been a lot of snickers behind my father's back when the word about Mrs. Bellamy got around. Maybe marrying Lil was partly designed to make up for that.

"A looker? Well, not for the last forty years, I'd say, although maybe she was all right when she was young. No, somebody you know," I said. "Mrs. Rutherford. From Point Loma."

He laughed. "The high school teacher?"

"The very one. She told me you'd moved here actually. She keeps track of a lot of her old students." I said, watching his face carefully.

He was my last connection to those days, and every time I came to visit, I tried to find out what he'd heard about Annie. I knew that they'd kept in touch, and I needed to know if anyone had said anything that might get back to Caroline and ruin my life. I never asked outright, and he never appeared to set out to tell me straight. But I'd gotten important information over the years from him.

He just grinned at me, though. "Well, Mrs. Rutherford should be tough enough to meet your dad halfway. My mother always said that your mother had a lot of backbone ..."

Then Richie hit a bug in the game and started squealing. Gus wheeled over to see what was happening: flashing lights that should have meant death to the explorer but that were just a dead end. "What you're going to have to do now ..." he began. Then when Richie had successfully navigated to a new level in the game, Gus turned his chair back so he could look at me. "That's just the sort of stuff I want to find out," he said. "You don't learn anything unless you make mistakes."

I nodded, not sure if there was anything I should read into the statement. "The game is very clever," I said.

"Pays the rent," Gus said. "Actually pays a lot more than that." And he smiled again. "Let me show you what I'm working on now," he said, rolling over to a bigger computer. "Weather," he said. "The games stuff is only for fun, but I think I've got something going here, looking at wave propagation. I'm working with some guys at Scripps." And I listened to what he had to say while the boys played on. They didn't want to leave when Caroline came for us, they would have stayed another two hours.

That visit had been more than ten years earlier, and for years afterwards I'd awakened in a panic once every month or so, sure that Lil had connected the dots running from Gus to Annie to me.

But now there Lil was, waiting for me in front of the house, our old house, my mother's house. Older, much older, a widow who no longer had the strength to live on her own.

Suddenly I knew why I had had such an easy time finding the complex. Lil had not mentioned it, perhaps she had not considered it important, but the complex was where Gus lived, where Annie worked, and I'd been there before.

The woman in the pickup whose voice had upset me had been Annie, of course.

I felt dizzy, I stumbled as I tried to step toward Lil. My knees buckled under me and I had to grab hold of the car door.

Lil laughed. "And what have we here? You've been drinking already this morning? Like father like son?"

"Hey, no," I said, struggling to pull myself together. My knee hurt, my heart pounded. "It's just been one hell of a trip. But I'm here. Let me get my stuff inside and give me forty-five minutes to take a nap and we'll get right on top of things." Nevertheless, when she moved closer to me I leaned on her as we went up the walkway to the house.

The sign in front said, "Sold." I whispered the word to myself ten minutes later when I lay on the bare mattress in my old room, trying to slip into sleep. "Sold." Another way of saying "the end." Which this might be. For something.

~

Annie

~

F*or the better part of two hours* that Sunday morning the doctors worked on Will. Chuck sat next to me in the waiting room outside the emergency room, fiddling with his keys the way he does when he's upset, while I stared out into space as all sorts of memories swirled around in my head. But then the waiting got to be too much for him, and he stood up. "Can't stand the uncertainty," he said, looking at me a little sheepishly. "I've got to have a cigarette. I'll go outside and see if I can bum one from someone." He leaned over and kissed me on top of my head. "I won't be but a few minutes."

Ordinarily I would have got after him about that, because if there's anything that's proven to be bad for you, it's smoking, and Chuck is a man I don't want to lose any earlier than necessary. I've gotten him to be more careful when he's working with the chemicals he uses for his landscaping business, he always wears gloves and sometimes other gear. I thought I'd convinced him about the smokes, too. But I understood how this was bothering him. I'd already bought myself a couple of chocolate bars, too, and I know I shouldn't eat them.

When he came back I was finishing up the second bar, and he pointed to it and grinned. "Sinners, both of us," he said. Then his grin froze, like he was remembering that sin was supposed to be punished, and the worse kind of punishment was suffering children. But he didn't say anything. He just sat down and changed the subject: "Did you get a chance to look at the mail yesterday?"

I hadn't. I'd worked the Saturday shift too in order to make sure I had both Christmas Day and New Year's Day off. "Anything interesting?" I asked, just to say something, because sitting there and worrying was pressing down on me so hard.

"The tickets," he said.

The tickets. I shut my eyes. I'd forgotten about the trip, but I knew that whatever happened now would have an effect on it, and on what Chuck had been planning for a long time. No wonder he'd wanted to go out for a smoke, this was an added worry.

The trip was his idea. We'd been married twenty-five years the fall before — no big deal, we'd both been busy, no time for a major celebration, just a meal in a restaurant. But a week afterwards he'd said, "What would you say to a real trip to celebrate our anniversary and to greet the millennium?"

I thought he was crazy, what with all the Y2K business, all the talk about how the world might grind to a halt at 11:59 P.M. on December 31, 1999. Everybody was running around, updating this, changing that, worrying that the machines we'd come to depend on were going to stop, all of them, all at once. Looking back it seems silly — nothing happened, all the changes had been made, and since then a whole lot of worse things have upset our lives, which have nothing to do with not enough zeros in computer programs. But then folks were afraid that airplanes would fall out of the sky as soon as the clock ticked the new millennium in.

"No, no," Chuck had said. "Nothing like that is going to happen, and besides, what I'm talking about is a trip that would have us on the ground at the witching hour. It'd be a lot of fun."

He was persuasive, he had his arms around me when he told me that, and he was whispering into my ear.

"So where do you want to go? San Francisco or some place like that? Las Vegas?" I asked. We had some extra money, Reed's Gardening Experts had just got a big contract for maintenance at three shopping centres owned by a property management company.

"Nah," he said. "That sounds pretty tame. I was thinking ..." he paused and nuzzled me again, "I was thinking it would be cool to be at the first New Year's celebration."

"The first," I repeated. New York? London? "What do you mean, the first?" I asked.

"I mean the first, some island in the Pacific, just on the other side of the International Date Line. New Zealand, maybe."

I twisted around in his arms so I could look at him. "You're nuts! New Zealand?"

"Yeah, why not? And then," he continued before I had a chance to react, "since we're already out there, maybe we could go to Australia and have a look around."

I didn't say anything. I couldn't say anything. I'd been to Tijuana, but I'd never been any other place outside California, let alone outside the U.S.

"You know how much of the stuff that we grow here comes from there: maybe a third of all the ornamentals. I'd learn a lot of stuff that would help Reed's Garden," he said, and so I knew that this wasn't just a wild hare. He'd been thinking about it for a while.

But I couldn't look at him while I tried to get my mind around the idea. He put his index finger under my chin and lifted my face to make it harder for me to avoid his eyes. "It'd be cool," he said again. "It's summer there now, everything will be in high season, we'd hit the big gardens, we'd look up a couple of contacts I've made over the years. You remember that landscape gardener who did the design for the hospital grounds? He always said to come see him ..."

"You can't just show up on people's doorsteps. It's Christmas time there too, he might be away for the holidays," I said. "Besides —"

But he didn't let me continue. "No, he'll be there. I wrote him a couple of weeks ago and he faxed me right back."

That made me look at him. His eyes were crinkled up with pleasure. "You said we were coming?" I asked.

He made a sort of nod that could have been yes, could have been no, but then he added the clincher. "The tour people I spoke to said we could make a side trip to Vietnam too."

And then I saw where all this was leading. The bad stuff about the Vietnam War still haunted him, he woke up screaming at least three times a year with nightmares that he wouldn't or couldn't put into words. But there was more. He was just a kid from Kentucky when he went to Vietnam and it was the first time when he'd lived in a really different landscape. He was amazed by all the tropical lushness, the bamboo and orchids and vines. When I met him he was even trying pick up a little French so he could read a second-hand book about Vietnam's plants he'd found, which had been published when Vietnam was a French colony.

"You want to see what's it's like now," I said.

"Yes," he said. He dropped his hands from my face and turned away, looking out the window at our own garden, which he'd constantly worked on weekends and evenings since we'd bought the place ten years before. He jingled his keys in his pockets, the way he always did. "I want to see what they've done with their gardens, I'd like to see how they fared ... I read this article in the paper about a guy who went back ..." He turned to look at me. "He said it buried some ghosts for him."

"I'll think about it," I said.

It took me about three weeks to go over the pros and cons, and to give him credit, he didn't bug me. We couldn't leave before Christmas, I wanted to have everybody over for dinner the way we always did, we couldn't change that. I called a couple of travel agents to ask just how risky travel would be over the new year, I even wrote a letter to the "Answer Man" column the newspaper was running as part of its Y2K stuff. They agreed: there might be some upset on New Year's Day, but given all the preparations things would be fine after that. If we didn't move from Wellington, or wherever, until January 2, we should have no problem.

So I said all right, and Chuck made the reservations. To bury some ghosts.

But I couldn't say anything more about the trip while we sat waiting for news about Will. "We'll talk about it later," I said. "You understand, don't you?"

He nodded his head yes. "Of course," he said. And then he sat down and put his elbows on his knees and looked around him while he worked his mouth like he tasted something bad or he wanted to cry.

Two other families were also sitting in the space set aside for worried friends and relatives down the hall from the entrance to the operating theatres. Emergencies of course — you don't do elective surgery on Sunday. One Latino family with an old grandmother saying her rosary, a pretty woman about Will's age who I guessed was the wife, and a half-dozen others who came and went. The other group was made up of another youngish woman who sounded like she came from New York or New Jersey or some place back east, and two men about the same age who didn't look related: the wife of some Marine stationed at Camp Pendleton and his buddies, I figured. Violent accidents: car crashes, fights, knifings.

Like Will.

Who was being operated on.

For a moment Chuck and I both sat there, thinking about him and what he meant to both of us. Once long ago I had asked Chuck if he ever regretted not having a son of his own, and he said, "What do you mean? Will is my son far more than he ever was any other man's." *For sure*, I thought then.

Now, however, Chuck seemed to decide that he couldn't let us sink too far into our sorrow, like he knew there was more to come and we needed to keep our spirits up. He looked over at me and picked up my hand again. "I put the tickets in the freezer," he said. "For safe keeping."

For just a second I stared at him, because I was so deep inside my worry. But then I knew I should laugh because I loved Chuck too. "Where every thief knows to look, first thing," I said. I put my arm around his shoulder and leaned my head against his solid, comfortable body.

He chuckled once, softly, deep in his throat as if he had to force the little laugh upward. "Oh, I don't know if we have to worry about being robbed. Everything can't go wrong all at once."

"Shh," I said, "don't say that. It's tempting fate." Then I noticed that the clock on the wall said it was nearly noon. "Listen, when you were out did you call the girls?" I asked. If he hadn't, we ought to. They'd both be up by now, and they'd want to know.

"No," Chuck said. "I thought about it, but then I said, wait until we know what's up. And there's Meredith: she doesn't know either, does she?"

Will and Meredith had been an item for three, maybe four years. She was a smart cookie, she worked for a bank, and even though she hadn't done much college, she was heading up one of those teams preparing for Y2K. Once the millennium had arrived, she and Will were going to get married, but until then she was working seventy hours a week. Her mother had been looking after her little boy most of the time lately, and I didn't have any of their phone numbers.

"I wonder if Will had his cell phone on him. He's probably got her numbers programmed in," I said. If I asked around I might be able to find out. So far I hadn't seen any familiar face on the staff, but that didn't mean there wasn't someone who knew someone who knew someone I knew. That always helped when you wanted a favour. "I'll go talk to the nurse at the desk. Maybe she can find out what's happening too."

"No, Babes, don't bother about Will's phone," Chuck said, standing up. "The girls will have Meredith's phone number. I'll call them, and they'll call her. They'd do a better job in breaking the bad news anyway."

True. I nodded yes, and stood up too so I could put my arms around him. He smelled comfortingly of grass and machine oil and himself underneath the cigarette smoke. I felt tears well up in my eyes, and I wished that this day was past, that we were through whatever trial lay ahead and were home in our bed, and he was there to protect me from the evils in the world.

But he couldn't. Before he had found a phone to call Kimberly and Margaret, the surgeon in charge came out of the operating theatre and motioned us to follow him into a little office off the waiting room. He made sure we were sitting down and then he stood, leaning against the door. "I'm very sorry," he said. "With such a strong young man I thought we had a chance. But he's gone."

~

Rick

~

I *ought to address the matter of* emotion, as Jenny would put it. Emotions, she says, are an important component of human behaviour. They are useful, they are what protect us, what goad us into action when we are threatened, what lead us into relationships with others. But expressing them has its pitfalls, because in our society and in our intimate relationships, inappropriate emotional behaviour can be counterproductive. Yet repressing emotions is not good either. Control them, channel them, manage them, she always says. Use that energy to an end you choose for yourself, don't let it overwhelm you.

I can see her saying all that in front of the family law class she teaches at the community college, making her pitch for mediated settlements and enlightened regulations. I sat in on the class once when we first started going out, waiting for her so I could take her to dinner afterwards. Her words made a lot of sense; the mess Caroline and I had made for ourselves crossed my mind, but at that point I was more interested in the pretty mouth that was saying the words and the little smile Jenny gave whenever she said something that was particularly tough.

She's tough. She's little and beautiful and tough, and she nearly always keeps her emotions under control. Whatever I know about myself, I learned from her. I owe her a lot. It hasn't been easy, let me tell you, and working in a kitchen has both helped and not helped.

On the negative side, kitchens are crazy. You're run off your feet. You can't hesitate, you have to act, you're operating on nerve alone. Take a look at my hands and you'll see. I have scars from burns and cuts all over them, and I couldn't even tell you how I got half of them because I was so pumped at the time that I didn't notice. I actually lost the tip of my left index finger, half the first joint, without feeling it. I'd been de-boning chickens frantically when our supplier screwed up and we had to substitute and I was so mad I wasn't aware what happened until the guy who was supposed to be cleaning up after me saw the blood pooling around the carcass. I just about went ballistic about that one, because I should have tossed everything my blood had touched, and we still were without a special for the day, and I had to go to the emergency to get the finger stitched back up.

But on the positive side, I'm finally doing something I want to do, for myself. I'm following my own script at last, and the people around me — Jenny and Cassis particularly — support me. I've come to terms with the underlying reasons for my emotional landscape.

I wasn't always so quick to react to things that happen to me, though. In fact, the first time I ever remember being transported by emotion was when I was seventeen. I suppose I must have screamed a few times when I was little; children do. I see Cassis and her friends who get so angry that they cry over silly things, and I remember how Richie lay down on the pavement one afternoon when he was two and refused to walk one step further. I suppose I must have done things like that when I was very young. But when I was older, when I really had something to be upset about, I went along with the things that people wanted me to do. I didn't protest going to boarding school, I wasn't difficult when my mother got sick. Even when she died, even when my father hustled me out of town before high school graduation, I didn't rebel.

Maybe I should have. I've often wondered, lately particularly, what would have happened if I'd just left, gone to stay with Gus's family, refused to do what my dad wanted. But I didn't.

No. What I remember feeling was nothing. It was as if I were empty inside, like an inflatable toy, with no weight, at the mercy of every wind that blew. There were times when Annie and I were out on the cliffs that it seemed as if holding on to her was the only way to keep myself on the ground, to stay in contact with the world.

Gus called me the day after Mother's funeral service — he and his parents had been there — and asked if I wanted to go surfing that afternoon. It was Sunday, my father was still in his bedroom, the housekeeper wasn't supposed to come in until late afternoon, and my aunts and uncles had fled. There was no reason for me not go, nobody would even miss me. So I took my father's car, leaving a note to say I'd be back for the dinner that everyone in the family was supposed to attend before we left in the morning.

By the time I got to Flynn's in Ocean Beach, where Gus still stored his extra board, the day had turned gorgeous. The fog had burned off and the sea and the sky blazed with the kaleidoscope of blues that my mother caught a few times in her watercolours. (I remember how pleased she was when she'd get the right blend of paints: she'd call me over even though I'd be busy making digging a moat or watching the big guys or whatever. "Look," she'd say. "I just got close to God.")

The surf at OB was not good, though, and there were too many people, so when Gus said we should head back toward Sunset Cliffs, I didn't protest even though I had hoped to get further away from home. It was low tide and the beach called North Garbage looked better than South, so we climbed down the trail to it and then paddled out.

I was certainly a lot better at it than I had been in the fall, and being with Gus meant that I belonged. Nobody was going drop in on me, try to take a wave away from me. No one would question my right to be there. It was good to belong for once.

When we got beyond the breaker line, we just sat there for a few minutes, taking stock of the surf. There were a dozen other guys out, rocking up and down with the swell, waiting. From the water you could see the rooflines of a half dozen houses on that stretch of Sunset Cliffs Boulevard. Not our house, thank goodness. It was too far to the north and back a couple of streets. But Annie's was visible, and I tried not to look at it.

She hadn't come to the funeral, but then I had told her not to. I had told her I would call her, too, but I hadn't. I didn't know what I was going to do about her.

No, I didn't want to look at her house, yet I couldn't keep myself from trying to see if there was any sign of life there. Three cars were parked in the circle drive, but given the number of cars her family had, they didn't necessarily mean anyone was home.

Gus noticed where I was looking. "Checking out Annie's place?" he asked.

I remember grunting noncommittally. One part of me didn't want to talk about her with Gus, wanted to keep the moments she and I had had together untouched and perfect. Another part was ashamed and confused about what I should do next. I had to talk to her again, but I didn't have the words.

Gus wasn't going to let me get away with avoiding the subject. Maybe he was trying to cheer me up by joshing me. Maybe he sensed something more. I don't know. All I know is that a grin spread across his face. "Nice kid," he said. He was watching me to see how I'd react. "Great legs," he said. "Nice ass."

For a second I listened to his words repeat in my head, like an echo, like a drumbeat designed to force some thought deep into your brain. Great legs, nice ass. Both were true, but I couldn't allow myself to think about Annie in those terms. I continued to scull, to look back at the cliffs, at the house, at the places we had spent so much time recently.

She was not the first girl I had had. The year before when I was still at the boarding school, three of us had gone into Ojai and found a whore in the Mexican part of town. She had let us screw her for ten dollars apiece, one after the other, with a screen door the only thing between the quick rubbing of body to body and the hot afternoon outside.

I had not mentioned that experience to Annie: it seemed to have no relation to whatever was happening between us, to the way in which Annie was buoying me up, keeping me from drowning in sorrow. Yes, paradoxically, she may have been what gave substance to my empty being, but there were times when I lay on top of her in the hollows of the cliffs and I imagined myself floating over all these horrible days and nights because she was literally keeping me up. Then she was my life raft, my salvation.

She was, without a doubt, my first love in a time when I didn't want to love anyone because loving hurt too much.

But "great legs, nice ass"? No, I couldn't let Gus talk about her that way. She deserved better than that.

"Cut that out," I said. I turned on my board so I could face Gus. "Don't talk like that about her." The anger rose in me like storm surf. I began to paddle straight at him. "You say anything more like that and you die." In that moment I would have done him considerable damage, no matter how good a friend he was. Everything that had been bottled up inside came roaring out as I reached out to grab him, to strangle him, to punish him for what he'd said.

Gus was so surprised he didn't react immediately. With someone he knew had a short fuse he would have put up his arms immediately and prepared to flip him off his board. But he'd never seen me like this, and in the time it took him to realize just how angry I was, he lost the control that he usually brought to situations. "Hey," he said, paddling to the side and out of my way. "Come on, I was just joking, I didn't mean anything by it." Then he back-paddled suddenly so he was out of the range of my lunge. "Calm down," he said. "I think she's a really nice kid. Can't you take a joke?"

But I was on top of him, grabbing him from behind, letting my own board float free. I pushed Gus forward and to the left, aiming to get his head underwater. There was a long moment when he was completely submerged, but then he twisted free and jabbed his right elbow hard into my ribs. "Cut it out, you crazy son of a bitch," he shouted.

I suddenly found myself in the water, looking up at Gus who was poised for more action. I shook my head, to get my hair out of my eyes and to clear my head. Then I looked around for my board, swam the two strokes necessary to reach it and hoisted myself on it. I looked over at Gus. "Oh shit," I remember saying. "Oh shit, shit, shit. I don't know what I'm doing anymore. Do you think she'll ever forgive me if I go away?"

Gus was mad at me, I could see, but he didn't answer immediately. He paddled idly, looking around, watching the swell.

"Listen, you idiot, I don't know who you're really mad at, but I don't think it's me. You better not try a stupid stunt like that again with me."

A swell approached, it looked like it might be an all right one, but he let it pass. "If you don't want to go away, tell your father to fuck off," he said. "Move out. Get a job. You're nearly through with high school, you don't have to depend on him."

I couldn't look at him. "It's not that simple," I said.

"Life's not simple," he said. "Life's a beach."

I smiled: it was a new joke then. "Look, if I don't get a chance to talk to Annie before I leave, will you tell her good-bye for me?"

He stopped sculling and sat straighter on his board. "Listen, amigo, if she's so important to you that you try to kill me, do it yourself. You're a fucking coward if you don't," he said. Then he turned away from me and looked toward the swell. A wave was approaching, which he judged to be satisfactory, and he went for it.

I didn't. I sat out beyond the breakers for half an hour, trying not to remember that he'd called me a coward, pushing the anger down, watching to see if anybody came or went at Annie's. I saw no one, and it was a long time before I saw her again.

I did not say good-bye.

Nor did I ever tell off my father as I should have.

There was a period of several years much later when my rage was focused on Caroline. I broke a window once just before the end because I was so angry at her. But I never hurt the boys, I swear, and the only time I hurt her it was an accident.

Oh Jesus, I loved Caroline. I loved her for a long time. I remember when she wore nothing at all, when she would come to my apartment in Palo Alto and strip off her clothes immediately and stand in front of me with her hair hanging down over her shoulders, lovely shiny light brown hair and skin that was as smooth as silk. Even in Montreal she never wore anything in bed until Richie was eight months old and crawling. Then she started wearing nightshirts because when she'd bring him to bed with us to nurse in the early morning, he'd weasel around under the covers after he finished. That bothered her, she said.

I don't think that was a turning point, though. We did have Matt, after all, we slept together in the same bed for another eight years. No, I guess things started to unravel when she began sleeping in the basement, in the office we'd set up down there. She quit wearing makeup, she started putting on weight. Too much work for her classes to get exercise, she said, she had to get a draft of the thesis done, there was an article that was due, she didn't want to wake me up by crawling into bed so late when I had to get up so early.

So early: because by then she had me getting the boys off to school in the morning. Not that there was anything wrong about that, really. I do the same for Cassis now. Then it was just one more thing that pissed me off.

Particularly after the camping trip. Particularly when I had thought we might get our problems sorted out and we'd be able to start out over again in Kingston.

We went to there to look things over the third week in August because I had gotten the job offer from IBM the first of the month. I was pleased about it; I hadn't gone looking for it, it wasn't that much different from the kind of analysis I'd been doing for far too long in Montreal, first at the bank and then with the consulting firm. But I liked the idea that somebody had recognized that I was good at what I was doing, even if I hated it.

Caroline thought I was talking about Kingston, Ontario, at first, which she might have understood. Then when it became clear that I was talking about Kingston, New York, she said it was just a podunk town on the Hudson with nothing to recommend it. I argued that it was doing very well just then, that the Hudson River was much more picturesque than Lake Ontario, and that, damn it, I wanted to take the job.

On the third day of our discussion she finally agreed to come and look the place over. When we got there the people from IBM took us around and showed us the kind of properties for sale — much better value than what we could get in Montreal — and the day schools for the boys and the recreational possibilities and everything. I was impressed, I thought there was hope.

Then on the way back we stopped in the Adirondacks to camp in our van and to canoe. I'd planned it that way because Caroline liked canoeing and there was a nice little loop we could take through a half dozen streams and lakes. It was easy stuff, water that the boys could handle on their own if we were in the next canoe to come to their aid if the unexpected happened. *Look how nice it is here*, I planned on saying. *How can you not agree to move here?*

I'd been reading Matt the Narnia books then, and the water we slipped through reminded me of the end of *The Voyage of the Dawn Treader*. The Silver Sea that Lewis imagines isn't my Western sea, my Pacific Ocean, but it is wonderful nevertheless. It spreads out in front of Prince Caspian, with the shallows extending to the end of the world and the water lilies flowering and the light around above, below, inside.

These lakes, these streams were like that, and the boys seemed to catch the magic of the place. They had started the day by horsing around, splashing each other and trying to race us, but as we proceeded into the world of light and water, they slowed down and paddled silently. Dragonflies skimmed inches above the water, swallows chittered near the tops of the trees, the water lilies opened their hearts to the sun as if exposing the centre of the universe. I could not see Caroline's face because she was in the front of the canoe, but I imagined she felt the spell too.

I was wrong.

It happened that the trip coincided with our anniversary, and I had included a bottle of champagne, one of a good Merlot, and a flask of brandy in our supplies. What I wanted to do was barbecue something juicy over an open fire and then sit around in the twilight, drinking the wine and then the brandy until it was reasonably late. The boys would sleep in the little tent I'd brought for them, and we'd have the van to ourselves.

When they went to the communal bathrooms to get ready for bed that night, however, Caroline began talking about how she thought it would rain before morning. She didn't want the boys to get wet, she said. She didn't want them to catch cold this close to the start of school, she thought they should sleep in the van with us.

I remember looking up at the sky where the moon was shining in spite of a few wispy clouds flowing like silver around it. "You got to be kidding," I said. "Besides, the boys want to stay in the tent. It may be their last time this summer."

"Oh, they already had their wilderness experience, three weeks at camp is enough for anybody," she said. She stood up, she turned to pick up the empty bottle on the picnic table.

"Not if you're a boy," I said.

She turned around abruptly and frowned at me. "So it's a guy thing," she said. "Then why don't you sleep in the tent with them?"

"No," I said, and reached out to take her hand. She snatched it away but didn't say anything because the boys were back.

I herded them into the tent, and their flashlights made it glow like a Chinese lantern. Inside I heard Matt say he was tired, followed by a yawn from Richie. They didn't turn their flashlight off until I said "Lights out," of course. But inside of ten minutes their rustling stopped.

Caroline was already in the van. She didn't look up when I opened the door, just continued going through her bag, looking for something. I stepped across to her quickly and put out my arms to turn her toward me. She didn't react immediately, but when I started to slip my hands up under her sweatshirt, she pushed my arm away.

"No," she said. "Not tonight."

The campground was quiet. An owl called somewhere in the distance. A sudden breeze blew through the leaves.

"Yes, tonight," I said. She stood there, an overweight woman in a sweatshirt and sweatpants with her hair pulled back from her face. She had no makeup on, she didn't even have a smile. "Yes, tonight. It's our anniversary," I said.

She fought a little. "Get your hands off me, "she said.

"Shh," I said, "you'll wake up the whole campground."

"Stop it," she said. "Control yourself, you idiot." She pushed me away, she put her hands up to keep mine off her breasts.

But in the end she didn't resist much. I did rip the material of her sweatpants as I tried to slip them down, I admit, but I only hit her with my elbow when she tried to twist away.

When we got back to Montreal she announced that she and the boys would stay there while I "tried it out" in Kingston. Her words: tried it out.

That was more or less the end with her.

But that was years before, and when I woke up in San Diego after my little nap I knew this Sunday morning also marked an ending. The knowledge that I had been involved in something terrible lunged at me the moment I opened my eyes. I had to talk to Jenny to see what she thought I should do. I must call her, and then I must call the police. There was no question about that. But I'd get Lil organized first.

When I came out of the bedroom that had been mine long ago, it was not quite 10:00 A.M. in San Diego; it was three hours later back in Kingston. My knee still hurt with every step, but I'd found an old elastic bandage in my room, left over from a sprained ankle I had when I was twelve. Wrapping it tightly around my leg helped a little.

"Do you want to make yourself some breakfast?" Lil asked. "I still have some eggs and orange juice and bread for toast." She stood in the middle of the kitchen, leaning on her walker. She'd never liked to cook, and once I began training to be a chef, she assumed I'd do everything when we came to visit. Obviously now she couldn't do much even if she wanted to.

"Sure," I said, opening the fridge and taking things out. I had to stand on my left leg, because the right one hurt, but I told myself I'd have to put up with it. "What about you? What about an omelette?" There were also a desiccated piece of cheese, a withered onion, a small, unopened can of chopped olives, and a half-empty bottle of olive oil.

She smiled at me. "Oh dear, oh dear, that sounds wonderful. They tell me that the complex has very good food, for an institution, but I expect anything will be better than what I can cook." She paused. "Particularly these days."

I turned around to look at her. She was settling herself at the kitchen table, with her walker in front of her. There'd always been someone who came in and cleaned this house from the time of my mother, and during various periods, someone had cooked meals too. I think Lil also had nursing help every day when my dad fell ill. If she had decided to move she must be feeling even more vulnerable than she looked.

But I didn't ask. Instead as I cooked I told her about the Christmas program Cassis was practicing for and Jenny's recent win in the copyright case and the prix fixe menu for our millennium celebrations.

"I'd love to be there," she said. "Are you going to have music and dancing? I heard there will be fireworks displays all up and down the Hudson; will you be able to see them from your place?"

"Don't think so," I said. "Most of that stuff will be down nearer New York City. What kinds of things are planned for the complex?" Nothing had been taken out of the kitchen cupboards, I saw. She'd said she wanted me to take whatever I wanted, and that the movers were supposed to prepare my boxes for mailing so I could take them to the post office on Tuesday. But she wasn't going to be able to fit all this stuff in her new place. Had she arranged for a used furniture dealer to come for the rest? Were there other people coming in to get things later in the week too?

"... a reception on New Year's Day," she was saying. "I had my blue wool dress cleaned for it, and I've invited a few of my friends up. We want to go out to dinner that night, but so far we haven't found a good place nearby that still has reservations available."

"Same story everywhere," I said. I put her plate in front of her: not a great omelette, but it looked nice. Then I sat down and began eating mine: I suddenly was starving. "But before we get that problem solved for you, we've got to make sure you've got rules of engagement set up for the movers."

We'd made a dent by late afternoon: I knew which dishes and stemware should be packed up for Jenny and me, and what Lil wanted to keep. The furniture she would use in the apartment was labelled with red tape, the stuff for St. Vincent de Paul with yellow, and that which was promised to various friends had tags with the name of the person. What remained were the contents of my old closets; she'd made my dad go through my mother's things before she married him, and after he died, she'd cleaned out most of his. Progress had been made, but Lil said she needed to lie down for a little before we did any more.

Exhaustion rose in my own bones like the tide, while my knee, which I had been trying to ignore, suddenly began to throb. *I should sit down and unwrap it to make sure the circulation isn't cut off*, I thought. And then I would sit with a cup of coffee for a few minutes, with the leg on a chair and on top of my knee a pack made from the two trays of ice cubes that remained in the refrigerator. I should take a few aspirins, too. No, better yet, I'd look in the medicine chest in Lil's bathroom to see if she had some ibuprofen, because I seemed to remember that it was good for sprains and stretched ligaments.

The doorbell rang as I was reading the label on her bottle of sleeping pills (prescribed three years before, just after my father died, I saw). I didn't want the noise to disturb Lil so I hurried out. That bottle and my little flask with my aspirin and my uppers were still in my hand when I opened the door.

"Richard James Mercer?" said a man in a sheriff's uniform. "We have a few questions for you."

~

Annie

~

"*What do you mean, Will's gone?" Chuck* roared at the young doctor. "What do you mean, you're sorry?" His voice shook, he was so angry. "What you mean is that my stepson died on the operating table because some bastard knifed him." He stood up and took a step toward the doctor. "You mean that you guys didn't get him to the hospital quick enough to patch up his lung or whatever. Just what the hell is going on?"

The doctor looked even younger than Will. He put his hand up over his face as if to deflect Chuck's scorn. "I'm sorry," he repeated. "We're sorry."

Chuck looked over at me. "A lot of good that will do," he said.

I shut my eyes. Your children aren't supposed to die before you. They are supposed to see you into your old age, arrange for your care, visit you on holidays, give you grandchildren, carry on the flame. They aren't supposed to leave you on a Sunday a few weeks before Christmas. They are supposed to live into the new century, the new millennium, and make it their own.

Chuck came over to me and put his arm around me, pulling me to him, so I could hide against him if I wanted to. I leaned into him. I did not think I could ever open my eyes again. Tears welled up behind my eyelids and spilled out over my cheeks, scalding hot. I tried to wipe them away with my fingers, but they came too fast. I held my breath, as if that would help.

I don't know how long we stayed there. At some point the doctor must have left. There were noises: doors opening, doors closing, someone calling someone on the intercom, Chuck coughing and then blowing his nose. But I was somewhere else. I can't say where, I don't remember. I was reaching, perhaps, to touch Will's spirit as it left us.

I've seen a lot of folks die, probably a good two dozen. I've been beside a couple of hundred others minutes after they sighed and died, or cried out and died, or grew rigid with pain and died. You do not work for twenty-five years in nursing homes and not become familiar with death. Most of the time I think it is a sort of door opening into a room we cannot see or imagine. But I could not think that comforting thought when the dead one was my only son.

"I'm sorry to disturb you," a woman's voice said, as I heard the sound of a door opening again.

"Yes?" Chuck replied, his voice thick. "What do you want?"

I opened my eyes. A woman in light pink scrubs with a nameplate and a clipboard. "You are the parents?" she asked. "We have some questions. There are some formalities."

The formalities are what keep folks going: notifying others, arranging funerals, finding wills, looking for documents, cleaning out drawers. Reading old letters, telling stories, picking up the pieces. Somebody has to do these things; they make you start to move again, they push you away from the door that leads to the room beyond.

I knew that. I'd seen the inevitable question about what to do with the body bring life back to eyes that were sunk in sadness. Sometimes the answer is easy — the dead person had said, or the living have definite ideas. Other times it means wrangling and more tears, shouts and slammed doors when those left behind do not agree. But nearly always it starts the wheels turning again.

Probably it would have moved me, if Chuck hadn't been there and if the question hadn't been different from the usual one. We couldn't do anything with Will's body right away, because it was a criminal case. An officer from Homicide would have to come, and then the County Medical Examiner. There'd be an autopsy, and burial or cremation would have to wait until that was done. Chuck had to tell the girls and Meredith what had happened, but he couldn't move us to the next step of planning a memorial yet. What he did immediately was begin talking about "getting the bastard who did it."

That afternoon I followed him around, because I did not want to let him out of my sight, because I could not think what else to do, because my eyes were open but saw nothing but Will lying in the parking lot. I am sure someone told me how Gus remembered seeing a bright blue Neon roaring down the road from the top of the mesa just before he found Will, but I have no recollection of that. Once the Sheriff's Department got the word that Will was dead, they shifted their investigation. What had been assault became a possible murder, and Gus's glimpse was the strongest lead. They sent word to the Department of Motor Vehicles to find out who owned all the cars like that in the state. They alerted all law enforcement agencies and the Mexican border stations. They told Chuck that it could be worse, because that colour of paint was so new that probably only six or seven thousand cars in Southern California had it.

Six or seven thousand? Chuck said that was small comfort, and he decided to get the word out himself. When we went back to the complex to talk to the detectives and to pick up my things, Gus said Chuck should use his office to make calls. So first Chuck broke the news to Kimberly, who said she would call Margaret and the two of them would go to Meredith's place to stay with her for a while.

Then he called the television stations and the newspapers. It shows just how upset he was that he was able to do that. He's a man whose only contact with the media to that point had been putting an ad for Reed's Garden Experts in the yellow pages. But at KPYC, the first station he called, he was put through to the news editor, and it must have been a slow Sunday, because the man listened to Chuck's story about how an innocent, good-hearted young man had been cut down for no reason in the parking lot of convalescent hospital. Who did it? Chuck wanted to know. How can justice be done? Then, once that station ran an item in midafternoon as a teaser for the 5:00 P.M. local news, the others jumped on the story.

Meredith was furious when the KPYC crew showed up on her driveway in the middle of the afternoon, even though she knew Chuck meant no harm to her. He just wanted to make sure that the word got out, even though I might have wanted to talk him out of starting a crusade if I'd been able to think more clearly.

But I wasn't, I wasn't there in any sense that mattered. If you look at the pictures that the newspaper photographer took, you'll see me with my hair coming down and my shoulders slumped. I look like one of our patients, somebody who's had a stroke and who finds that moving is almost more than she can do.

In the end, though, it wasn't the news bulletins and the descriptions of the blue Neon that found the man who killed Will. It was the fact that the Sheriff's Department contacted car rental agencies when they showed up as owners of about fifty blue Neons. When the sheriff had the names of who had rented them, the deputies started tracking the drivers down. Did any of the names mean anything to anyone at the complex? They asked everyone.

Chuck saw no name he recognized, and no one asked me because I was so very out of it. But Gus and the complex staff saw Richard James Mercer III, whose stepmother was scheduled to move into the complex that week.

Bear in mind that Will would never have been born if things back then had been like they are today. The Pill works, abortion is legal, and like I always told my girls, if you can't be good, you can be careful.

Then it was much harder. The Pill was around, but you had to make an appointment with a doctor to get a prescription, and it didn't occur to me to do that. I suppose R.J. could have used condoms, he must have known about them, all the boys did. But it wasn't like now when you go into a drugstore and there's a display of them, back then you had to ask someone to get them out from behind the counter. It was embarrassing, an admission that you intended to do something you shouldn't be doing.

As for abortion, well, a few years later I knew someone who went to Tijuana to a real doctor who performed one in his office under sanitary conditions. But I didn't know about that sort of thing then.

Initially, when my mother asked questions about my periods and my vomiting, I brushed her off. I couldn't be all that pregnant, I figured, so I had a little time to decide what to do. Most importantly, I had to talk to R.J.

But he did not call, and nothing came in the mail from him. By the second week after he left, I decided I had to ask Gus for help. He of all people would be most likely to know how to contact R.J., and he would understand best.

So I tried to call him — his phone number was listed, his family didn't have any reason to pay extra in order to hide — but his mother said he was spending most of his time at the beach. So I went looking for him, first at North and South Garbage across from our house on the cliffs, and then, when he wasn't there, at Ocean Beach.

It was early afternoon, the sun had burned off the fog, and he was sitting on his board beyond the line of breakers, along with ten or so other guys surveying the surf. Afterwards I had to go to work at the bakery where I'd found a summer job, so I was wearing a black skirt and a white blouse, which made me stick out from everyone else stretched out in bathing suits. But I couldn't let that bother me. I took off my shoes at the edge of the sand and walked barefoot toward the water

Gus saw me when I waved at him, and waved back. Then I started gesturing for him to come in, but he hesitated for a few moments before making a move. I saw somebody say something to him, and I was sure it was a remark about how uncool I was or some such thing. But no matter, he seemed to realize it was important and he caught the next wave.

I waded out toward him. I felt stupid, holding my skirt up above my knees so it wouldn't get wet and clutching my shoes to my chest.

"What's up?" he asked as soon as he was close enough to be heard above the waves.

"I've got to talk to you," I said. "Can we go for a walk along the beach or something?"

Gus glanced up at the encampment of girls further up the beach, checking out who would watch him go for a walk with me. Not that it mattered, really. He nodded. "Just let me park this," he said.

I followed him up the beach, but stood back when he put the board down next to the boards of a couple of other guys. Then we walked a half a football field down the beach before I told him what the problem was.

First, though, I asked him if R.J. had been in touch with him since he left.

He shook his head no. "But his father's back," he said. "My mother saw him taking the housekeeper to the supermarket last week. She talked to him; he still looked pretty broken up."

I nodded, and walked on in silence for a couple of minutes. The waves splashed up against my legs, getting my skirt wet. There'd be white salt marks on it, but no matter. "I can imagine it must be hard for Dr. Mercer," I said. "But it's got to be pretty tough for R.J. too. I ... I … I ..." I stammered, I didn't know quite how to put it.

"He didn't want to go," Gus said. "He told me that he didn't want to leave you."

My heart took a jump at that. That was the kind of thing I wanted to hear. "He did? Good. But look, I've really got to talk to him." I stopped and put out my hand so he'd stop too. We were nearly to the rocks at the end, in the place where they were going to build the fishing pier, the part of the beach where the old folks liked to sit and watch the waves.

"What do you want to talk to him about?" Gus asked.

"I'm pregnant," I said.

"Shit. Pregnant," he said. "Shit."

"I've got to tell him," I said. "My mother has begun to talk about how I have to get married."

"Married to him?" he asked. He looked at me sharply. A few people in our class had already gotten married, a couple of girls had disappeared to have babies, but none were people either he or I knew well.

"I'd like to," I said.

Gus turned around and started walking north on the beach.

"If I don't hear from him, my mother is going to insist that I tell his father," I said.

"She knows?" he asked.

"She suspects. She's furious that I won't tell her more, she says I'm acting like a slut." I started to cry. It was so unfair of her to say that, I had only loved him, I had only tried to comfort him. "She says that if it's true, his father is going to have to make him get in touch with me."

"And it's true? And you want to talk to him without his father getting involved?"

Of course I did, why would you want to bring parents into it? Why would you want to do what they decided was right?

But Gus couldn't help. "Sorry," he said. "I wish I knew where he was. He said something about Montana, but that's a pretty big place."

So in the end my mother called his father, and we had a council of war without R.J., because R.J. had already started on the brilliant career his father had always planned for him.

Dr. Mercer said as much. We couldn't expect a boy like R.J. to be tied down at this point in his life. It was too soon after his mother's death anyway. If R.J. had behaved in an ungentlemanly fashion toward me, well, there would be compensation. But any further contact between him and me was out of the question.

I've wondered since why he didn't just arrange for me to have an abortion; surely he knew which medical men did such things. Perhaps he had principles of a sort, maybe he did believe in the sanctity of life.

As for my mother, after that terrible evening when she and I and Danny sat around our kitchen table, she never mentioned it again. She thought she was doing the best thing for me, I've decided. She didn't think I'd be happy with R.J., she thought he'd be ashamed of me and we wouldn't last. Maybe she was right, but Danny and I didn't last either.

And Danny was duped. No, that's not quite right. Maybe it's better to say that Danny chose not to know. He touched my hand as he listened while my mother explained the situation: the baby would be born sometime in the winter, it would need a father, and I had told my parents about his visit, his attack, his rape. There was a certain amount of money earmarked for me, and we could use part of it to set up housekeeping if we got married now. If not, well, Danny knew how my brothers were. Even if he and they had always been friends they'd react in certain ways, once they knew what Danny had done and what he'd then refused to do.

"You don't need to threaten me," Danny said. He sat up straighter, he took my hand in both of his. "Of course we'll get married." So he bought the pickup, he allowed his name to be on Will's birth certificate. And, at least as far as I knew, he never counted from April to February when Will was born, or noticed the unusual colour of the baby's eyes.

That's all water under the bridge, of course, and nobody ever knew the truth except my mother, Dr. Mercer, Gus, me, and R.J. Yes, in the end R.J. found out because when he finally wrote to Gus a couple of years later, the year I decided I had to go it alone, Gus wrote back and told him.

I almost told Mrs. Rutherford too, even though it was too late by then for her to say anything. She came in the bakery where I was working toward the end of August, when I was sitting on the high stool at the cash register, catching a couple of minutes of rest. My feet and ankles were beginning to swell, I had to pee all the time, and I could sleep standing up. Danny liked how big my breasts were becoming, and my belly hadn't yet begun to repulse him. He wanted to screw every night, and I let him, although sometimes I was asleep before he finished.

Mrs. Rutherford seemed surprised to see me even before she saw that I was pregnant. "Well, hello," she said. "And how was your summer? All ready to start college?"

Those were questions I couldn't answer, so I avoided them. "It's good to see you. How may I help you?" I said, taking care to say "may" not "can" because she had been so very adamant about the difference between them.

But she didn't notice because she was looking around the shop. The display cases near the cash register held the cookies and cupcakes. The one along the wall had cakes, pies, and Danish pastries. "It must be a great temptation to work here," she said. "I'd always be wanting to try things." She smiled again and waited for me to say something. I knew I should laugh and make an offhand remark like, "Well, you get used to it, it's a job like any other." And then I should add that besides, I'd be starting at State or City College or wherever in a couple of weeks and ...

But of course I couldn't say that. So I just stood there, smiling, feeling fat and foolish.

Mrs. Rutherford waited for me to tell her about my future. She seemed to be listening carefully, the way she did when we were reading our essays, our stories, our poems. Other noises filled the afternoon, however: the murmur of the fan mounted on the wall, the voices of two boys shouting on the street, a car passing. Then when it became clear that I was not going to say I was looking forward to school in the fall, she sighed and then asked, "What do you recommend? I need something for dessert because I've got guests coming for dinner."

It was a question that could be answered without giving anything away. "The chocolate cakes are always popular," I said. "This size will give you eight servings, and this size will give you twelve." I bent forward so I could pull one of each size out for Mrs. Rutherford to see better. My belly made it awkward. She noticed, I was sure.

"The bigger one," she said. "I'll eat whatever's left over." Her eyes met mine, and she smiled. "I see you've gotten married," she went on, pointing to my left hand, but not looking at my belly.

I nodded.

"To anyone I know?" she asked. That was the moment when I could have told her, when I could have explained. But I didn't.

"I don't think so. He went to San Diego High," I said. "Danny Carlson is his name."

She nodded, and smiled again when I had finished putting the cake in a cardboard box. "Thank you," she said. "And, don't forget, if you ever want to talk to me about anything, my number's in the phone book."

In later years, I wondered what would have happened if our paths had crossed at the beginning of the summer instead of then, when everything seemed settled.

But they didn't, although when Will and I came down from the mountains and I was trying to figure out exactly what to do, I thought of her again. She wrote me the letter of recommendation I needed to get into the LVN program.

I never would have expected her to marry Dr. Mercer, though.

But then I never expected R.J. to kill Will.

~

Rick

~

T*he late afternoon sun outside was glaring* and I had to squint my eyes to make out the officers' faces. One was taller than me, maybe nearly six feet, while the other was a little guy, probably no taller than whatever the minimum height requirement was. He was the one who was speaking. "Mr. Mercer," he said, "is that your car in the driveway?"

I slipped the pill bottles in my right front pants' pocket, and I stood as straight as I could, considering my knee.

"I rented it this morning," I said. There was movement behind me, and in the mirror just inside the door I could see Lil's reflection. The doorbell had woken her up after all. She stood at the door between the hall and the living room, leaning on her walker.

"Rick, tell the gentlemen to come in," she said. She began to work her way forward, pushing the walker in front of her. She looked as if she were stiff from lying down, because she moved with much more difficulty than I had noticed earlier. "It will be more comfortable there for all of you."

I ignored her. I needed to set things up so that when I left with these men she wouldn't be alarmed. *I should have called Jenny sooner*, I thought. *I'm going to need a lawyer, no matter what has happened. How to find a good one here, when I knew so few people anymore?*

"We'd like to learn a little about what you did today, Mr. Mercer," the officer said. "That is your name, isn't it? Could we see some identification?"

I reached for my wallet in my back pocket and as I did I remembered where I'd left my knife. It wasn't the first time that day that I'd thought of how it had entered the man's chest, but earlier, when I'd been cutting and labelling for Lil, I had been able to push away the feel of the thrust and the look of the stricken man. It was not going to be so easy now. Whatever my reasons for heading straight to Lil's, it had been a mistake to run away.

"My stepson is forgetting his manners," Lil said. Her voice suddenly took on the authoritative tone of the good teacher. "Come in. Sit down."

If I hadn't been so worried I might have laughed at the officers' reaction. The tall one, who hadn't taken off his hat, quickly tucked it under his arm, and the other one squared his shoulders. "Thank you, ma'am," he said to Lil, looking past me. "But I don't know if we'll be staying very long." Then he began to examine my New York State driver's licence, which I held out for him.

"Look," I said. "Let's not bother Mrs. Mercer over this. Perhaps we could go outside in your car and talk. We've been working all afternoon, and I'm sure she needs to rest." Jenny probably wouldn't think much of me answering any questions no matter how innocuous without first talking to counsel, but what I was in, I realized, was damage control mode. My priorities were: one, protect Lil, and two, get the cops on my side.

The short deputy looked up at me to check my photo against my face.

"What is all this about?" Lil said. The authoritative tone was still in her voice, but when in the mirror I could see that her face looked older with worry.

"Something has happened ..." the deputy began.

"I suspect the officers want to talk to me about an accident I witnessed," I said, turning around and taking a step toward her. "Yes, an accident I witnessed early this morning before I got here." I was improvising, hoping for the best. "I didn't mention it because I didn't want to alarm you. But now that things are pretty well under control here, I should do what I can to help the investigation."

"An accident," she repeated. She looked at the officers, as if for corroboration.

"So," I said to the deputies, "let me get my jacket and I'll be with you." As I went past Lil I stopped to give her a hug. "Don't worry about me if you don't hear from me for a while. Order dinner in, and I'll get a message to you if I'm delayed."

Remember at this point I had no idea who the man I'd stabbed was, and I didn't want to think that he was badly injured. When I explained what had happened, they'd let me go, I hoped. If not, Jenny would see that everything worked out.

But I was not prepared for the two television crews outside on the street. When I opened the door I hadn't seen that a second and a third police car were blocking the street on either side of the house, so no one could get very close. A handful of people — neighbours? I had been around so infrequently I had no idea who lived nearby now — were watching from the far side of yellow police tape, and one of the TV vans was unfolding its remote satellite link antenna.

"What's the circus about?" I asked the taller officer, who opened the back door to their car. The TV cameras couldn't get too close but they were both positioned so they'd get me, full frontal. I hoped Lil wouldn't turn on the television while she waited to hear from me. Who knew what kind of crazy spin they might give to what was happening?

And then I heard what I didn't expect, what I hadn't allowed myself even to fear.

"Guy's been killed," the officer said.

Jenny was there by noon on Monday. When I called her, she told me not to say anything, to let them book me and put me in the holding cell, but to insist I had the right to remain silent until I had a lawyer of my choice.

"They don't look like they're going to like that," I said.

"So what? This is a situation that is completely absurd. You indicated your willingness to cooperate when you volunteered to go away with the officers. They can wait until you have proper advice." There was a pause, as if she were considering things. "You say it was an accident? That you panicked and blew it?"

"Yes," I said. I was as ashamed as I was worried. I'd let myself as well as everyone else down.

"Listen, big guy," she began. "You can't dwell on that. You've got to watch yourself. You've got to be cool. But I believe in you. Don't forget that."

I put down the phone, not feeling utterly lost. She would save me, as she had saved me before. I could even put up with a night in a holding cell, with nine or ten others and the smell of stale beer, vomit, sweat, and disinfectant if I had to. She would figure out a way to rescue me.

When we met, I did not think of rescue when I saw her. I thought of sex. It was in the spring of my first year in Kingston, when it had become clear that Caroline and the boys were never going to join me there.

That was traumatic. Jenny explained to me later that it's rare for a man to leave a marriage unless he's been kicked out or he's already found a substitute. Women will leave without a new man in sight in order protect children or because they can't take any more. But men like to go to something, they don't want to be cut adrift.

I don't know. I didn't push Jenny on where she got that information, because she sometimes gets touchy when I question her sources. Part of the lawyer's defence mechanism, I guess. Be aggressive if you aren't being believed. Whatever, I know that I was a lost man there for a while.

The job at IBM was okay, there was a lot of extra work, overtime, special projects, so I kept busy. I drank more than I should have, and between American Thanksgiving and the middle of March that first year I drove back to Montreal eight times to see the boys even though it was a bad winter and I was constantly slipping off the road going through the Adirondacks. But when it became clear that it was all over with Caroline, that she was going to get her divorce and everything else she wanted, I found I had a lot more evenings and weekends than drinking could fill. So for want of an excuse I agreed to play softball on an IBM team.

Jenny played for the courthouse gang. She was short and plump, wearing cut-off jeans and a big white shirt, with her curly black hair tied back in a ponytail. I thought she was probably somebody's secretary because she didn't look old enough to be a lawyer — and because, I admit, I didn't expect pretty girls to be lawyers themselves. She could hit too — hit a double in the seventh inning, but it wasn't enough for her team. We beat them, and then, because that was the informal rule in the league, we all went out for beer and pizza afterwards with the losers paying for the first round. I sat next to her in the pizza place, listening to her laugh at other people's jokes and wishing I could say something funny too. When she got ready to leave, so did I, which meant I was next to her when she got into her car to find that the battery was dead. A bit of luck for me, because she accepted when I offered to give her a ride home. To make a long story short, I was in love before she got out of my car.

We went to Europe on our honeymoon. By then the writing was on the wall at IBM, my job was scheduled to be cut in the next six months or a year — they shut down the whole installation in 1995. I told Jenny we had no choice but to start a new life.

That was a joke: her life was going quite nicely. She'd begun to specialize in intellectual property law, and she was keeping very busy. But she'd always wanted to see Italy, where her grandparents came from.

Neither of us liked what we saw of Italy, though. It was early August, and the hill villages we were supposed to visit were hot and dusty and the roads were full of crazy drivers. But our luck changed when we headed toward Cassis.

Lil insisted that we go there. She hadn't met Jenny at that point, she was officially neutral when it came to my marital life, although my father told me he was changing his will to settle money on the boys right away, since he couldn't trust me anymore when it came to them.

"You have always been irresponsible," he told me on the telephone; he'd called me at work, he didn't want either Lil or Jenny to hear. "From the beginning you have shown bad judgment. I thought Caroline would help you find your way, but I was sadly mistaken."

I let him talk. There was no point in protesting anyway. He could talk and talk and talk, and he never listened. When he was through, I told him that I had nothing to say and I said goodbye and I hung up. That was the right thing to do, Jenny said, when I told her. Be polite, but don't let yourself get sucked into an argument.

I didn't tell her that I went outside after the call, picked up a big rock from the landscaping in front of the building, and smashed the window of my car. "Locked my keys inside," I told the parking lot attendant when he came over to see what I was doing. "Didn't think about asking you," I added, when he said that he was good at jimmying windows.

Needless to say I got the window fixed before I drove the car around Jenny, and I never suggested what my father might have meant by "being irresponsible from the beginning."

So after our disappointment in Italy we headed for the little fishing village in France where Lil had spent a good part of the war. Beautiful, she had said, and she'd heard that it still was unspoiled.

We were skeptical all the length of the big highway that leads from the Italian border to Marseilles. The road runs back from the coast most of the way, and our guidebook said that was good because the coastal roads are so clogged in August. But there wasn't much charm about the highway. They're like airports: you've seen one and you've seen them all.

But then we turned off the main road and headed toward Cassis, and we saw that Lil had been right. My mother would have loved it, a lot of artists had. There are pictures by Signac and Dufy and others — I've got a couple of reproductions among my watercolours at Chez Cassis. And when we saw the high cliffs of the Falaise and the round harbour we were impressed. Of course it helped that a wind had sprung up, which blew away a lot of the air pollution, and that we found a hotel room quickly even though we didn't have reservations. A cancellation, it seemed; a sign, Jenny said.

The next day we ate breakfast on the terrace of the hotel, looking out at the fishing boats. The harbour was quiet; the air was fresh and smelled like what I remembered from home. I asked about hikes, and when the fellow at the hotel desk pulled out a little sheet with the trails to the various mini-fjords, called *calanques*, I knew I was going to have to convince Jenny to walk more than she was used to.

"But you must see the calanques, madame," the man said when she made a face at the idea of a hike. "You can go by sea, if you don't want to go on foot, but as for me, I prefer the walking."

Jenny looked at me, and when I stared back she agreed. So we bought bread, cheese, fruit, and wine, put everything in a day pack, and started out. We were early, it was cooler than it had been, and the first calanque turned out to be a little valley that opened directly on to the sea. It was no wider than you'd find where a stream had cut its way down the hillside in the hills behind San Diego, and that's really what it was, a stream-cut canyon flooded by rising water when the glaciers melted. The information sheet from the hotel said that people lived here during the Ice Age, and their remains have been found in the continuation of these valleys, which are now far under water.

"Cool," Jenny said. And she wanted to go on. But she was dragging when we got the next calanque an hour and a half later. It was all I could do to convince her to slog up the last bit of limestone hillside, past the sweet-smelling bushes — thyme, sage, heather, I don't know, but even more fragrant than I remember from the cliffs at home.

"It's supposed to be spectacular," I said.

"Sure, sure," she said. "I'm never going to move again." And then we came out to a flat place where we could see the blue-green waters of Port en Vau. The air was crystal clear and the sun was brilliant. I almost wept, thinking of what my mother would have done with the view.

We stopped to eat lunch at the Refuge du Piolet, a little hut at one of the best vantage points. After we'd taken off our shoes, and I'd massaged Jenny's feet, and we'd drunk half the wine, she said it was worth it. "Lovely, lovely, lovely," she said, curling up against me as we sat out of the wind. "Your step-mother was right."

I didn't say anything. I didn't want to think of Lil in this place because she reminded me of my father. What I wanted to do was find a way to stay in a place like this and do what I wanted to do.

Which was?

Which was get out of business, leave companies and critical paths and data analysis behind me, and do something creative.

Cook.

Run a restaurant where the food would be as good as this scenery.

We started back. The trail was more crowded, we saw people swimming in the calanques, the sun glittered off the sea.

"You know what I've been thinking," I said when we started down the last incline toward the town.

Jenny listened. Jenny didn't think I was crazy. She liked the idea, even. She remembered the culinary institute across the Hudson from Kingston (I had heard of it, but knew absolutely nothing about how you qualified as a chef). And she even knew of a couple of properties that might be interesting ones for the kind of restaurant I was talking about, old houses with beautiful views of the Hudson Valley. Her father's construction company would give us a good deal on any changes we wanted to make.

She believed in me. She worked as hard as I did to make the dream a reality: my second year at the CIA, when I was working crazy hours, she kept her law practice going and gave birth to Cassis and made sure that our life was as smooth as possible.

And when my father died, and didn't leave me what I expected, she said we should go ahead with the restaurant anyway. She got the bank loans and worked on the business plan and told me that I should let my anger die with my father.

She was right, of course. And I thought I had, I had tried to. But once again I needed Jenny.

The way it works is this: you have to be arraigned within forty-eight hours after you've been arrested, not counting weekends and holidays. Bail will be considered then, the charges presented. Which meant in this case that the Deputy District Attorney and the County Medical Examiner and the detective from the Sheriff's Department consulted on Monday afternoon about the charges. There were four main possibilities: first-degree murder (done with premeditation); second-degree murder (done during the commission of an "inherently dangerous act"); voluntary manslaughter (intentional, but done in the heat of passion); or involuntary manslaughter (accidental, but with criminal negligence).

Jenny was there for the hearing. Right after she got off the phone with me Sunday she took Cassis to her parents' place and caught the same red-eye flight that I'd taken the night before. But before she left she also talked to a couple of her criminal lawyer friends back home, and they found a lawyer in San Diego who'd take the case. (She couldn't because she's not a member of the California Bar.) He showed up at the Vista Correctional Facility, where'd they'd taken me early Sunday evening, and my deposition was made by midnight.

By which time the film clip of the cops picking me up at Lil's house had made it through four news cycles. When they took me back to the holding cell, two of the guys recognized me. "Hey, watch out, here comes a tough boy," one of them said, and the other one laughed. "Old but nasty," he said.

It wasn't the greatest night, I'll tell you. My knee was swelling, by morning it was as big as my thigh, and even though I asked for medical help nobody paid me any attention. I was in with some pretty tough guys because they separate the "dangerous" offenders from the ones who've been picked up for minor things. Two guys had been in fights where someone was seriously injured, and while the seven others didn't say much, they all looked very unpleasant. Not what I expected when I got off the plane not twenty-four hours before.

As I said, Jenny was there when they ushered me into the courtroom for the hearing. She was sitting with my lawyer, with her hair pulled back in a thick braid and her mouth slightly open. She often sits like that when she's waiting, as if she wants to be ready to jump into a conversation, or to smile when she makes a point. I like to kiss her when her lips are parted like that, when she's concentrating on something, when I can surprise her. I would have loved to be able to jump the barrier that marked off the prisoner's box and stride over to her and tell her there is no woman more interesting or fascinating or capable in the world.

But I couldn't. I had to listen while they decided my fate.

I'm told that usually in a case like mine the DA goes for the charge that looks "best," the one most likely to be proved. The medical examiner certified that death resulted from a knife wound to the chest, which perforated the lung and caused massive bleeding. My fingerprints were on the knife found in the victim's chest. The car I'd rented had been seen leaving the scene. I did not resist arrest but I had fled from the scene of the crime. And the victim — let this not be forgotten, it's important, it's what made all the difference, I think — was a fine man, much beloved by his family and associates.

The possible charges against me could have been either first- or second-degree murder or involuntary manslaughter, and it's here that the news coverage made a difference. In order to make an example of me, the DA decided to go for second-degree murder.

And what did I plead? Not guilty, of course. Self-defence. I thought I was being attacked. But at a hearing like that you don't go into detail.

The Probation Department had checked me out. No prior convictions, owner of property in New York State, family in San Diego County. But on the other hand the seriousness of the charges argued in favour of bail sufficiently high to insure that the defendant would show up for all court appearances ...

And of course that's what bail is, basically: just a bond that you'll show up. In California you have to put up 10 percent of whatever the amount is, and then a bail bond company will put up the rest, provided you've got property to sign over as guarantee. When the judicial process is over — when you are either cleared or convicted — title to the property comes back to you or whomever it belonged to before. But the up-front money is gone.

"This is a serious offence," the judge said after the probation officer finished his evaluation. "This is a man from the other side of the country, who, despite his roots here, has been involved in a very questionable affair. I see no reason to set bail low, particularly since it is clear that he fled the scene. That would not augur well for future court appearances were he freed on bail. One million dollars."

Then the bailiff hustled me out before I even had a chance to blow a kiss to Jenny, or see her wave at me.

And still I didn't realize who the victim was. William W. Reed meant absolutely nothing to me. Not even the shots on the TV news of the grieving family told me anything. Two overweight middle Americans who rode around in a van with Reed's Garden Experts on the side: the father had a country accent, the mother didn't say anything. I didn't even make the connection with the pickup I'd seen in the complex parking lot and its "ANNIE" vanity plates.

Lil might have put two and two together if she'd seen any pictures of Annie, but she was so involved in postponing her move and then in worrying about me that she didn't have time for more than a quick glance at the television news. She had no idea of the connection until she and Jenny went to the funeral.

Going had been Jenny's idea. "A gesture of respect," she told me on the phone Wednesday night, after Lil and Jenny had talked it over. They should go to sign the guest book, shake a few hands, and offer condolences, which would show "just how devastated we are too," Jenny said. "You are innocent. This is a tragedy for us as well as for them."

Tragedy? Yes, of course, the death of anyone is, and I could begin to see the defence that Jenny thought we ought to play: decent citizen, overworked and overtired, reacts instinctively to a perceived threat. But she, of course, had no idea just how deep the tragedy was.

Nor did I, until she called me up the evening after the funeral to give me a report on how it had gone. She'd picked up Lil at her house, where she was still living amid boxes that I'd helped her pack.

"She's such a feisty person," Jenny told me. "I said I'd take her home afterwards, but she told me that she didn't want me to have to worry about her. 'You've got enough to do, my dear,' she said. 'I can fend for myself.' And she went and found a ride home with the brother of that old friend of yours, Gus Fraser."

"Gus," I repeated, wondering a little.

But before I could ask anything, Jenny was onto the description of the church. You couldn't tell from the outside what denomination it was, because it was one of those new ones built since the north part of San Diego started to fill in, with a New England–style pitched roof, California mission adobe coloured walls, and red tile decoration. A mélange of architecture to go with a mix of theology, she said. Neither a conventional Protestant nor Catholic church, maybe some kind of Pentacostal.

When they got there it is was filling up rapidly, and by the time the service started, nearly all the eight hundred seats — canted like those in a theatre — were full. Neither Jenny nor Lil really expected to see anyone they knew, and they had planned to sit off to the side. But an usher took a look at Lil and her walker and led them down in front where the floor was flat. Three people in wheelchairs were already there, and Lil recognized Gus immediately.

"Angus Fraser," she said as she shuffled toward a regular seat. "How good to see you. What are you doing here?"

He recognized her too, Jenny said, and gave out a little whoop that hardly matched the way he looked, imprisoned in his motorized chair. She knew about him, of course. I'd mentioned him many times, but she'd never met him because, well, because since I married her I'd been concentrating on my new life so much that I didn't have much energy to keep up links with my old one. As well, I don't know how I would have played seeing him, because he knew so much. But neither Jenny nor Lil knew the half of it, and Jenny said she decided to be charming even before Gus knew who she was.

And this is where it gets so difficult.

"Of course your friend knew most of the people there," she told me. "The poor fellow who died worked at the complex where Gus lives, you see. So did his mother."

The hair on the back of my neck stood up, I felt something coming, but I didn't guess what.

"Both Lil and he said you probably remember her, she was in your high school class too."

Annie? But I didn't ask.

"Gus pointed her out to me, and her husband, and their daughters and a young woman with a small boy who were the poor dead guy's girlfriend and her son." Jenny was in full flight and I let her talk on while I struggled with what I was feeling.

Annie was that heavy-set woman on the TV news! Yes, there might have been a shadow of the girl in that woman.

Jenny was continuing: "The family all sat down in front, and behind them was a man who Gus said might have been Danny somebody, the poor guy's natural father, even though he'd been adopted by his mother's second husband."

Natural father. Second husband. Of course, Danny had married her, I'd known that. How old was the guy I stabbed, thirty-one, thirty-two? Just the right age to be Annie's baby, I knew without doing the arithmetic.

I was talking on the only working telephone in the prisoners' day room. There had been another, but it was broken because somebody had ripped the receiver off. How many horrible messages had been relayed on that telephone? How many dreadful truths had been revealed?

And now one of the worst possible was slowly sinking in: I had killed my son.

"What's her name?" I said, once I had caught my breath.

"Whose name?" Jenny asked; she was now talking about the U2 songs that were played before the service began.

"The guy's mother. What's her name again?"

"Annie Reed now, but she was Annie Wallace. Gus said to make sure I told you that."

"Jesus," I said.

"I introduced myself," Jenny was saying, "but I don't know that she even heard me. This must be a terrible time for her."

A terrible time, a terrible, terrible time.

"But Lil told Gus how awful you feel about it all, about what a tragic accident it all was. That's a message that ought to get passed on, don't you think?"

Oh sweet Jesus, I hoped so. I never wished that poor boy ill.

Annie's boy disappeared one afternoon of my second week back in San Diego the summer Caroline and I got married. I knew he'd been born by then, Gus had written me.

On that particular day Caroline and Mrs. Bellamy had gone shopping together. They were going to register us at all the department stores and at Jessops and the Linen Closet. Not at all necessary, it seemed to me, because Caroline's mother had done the same thing in Montreal for us. We risked getting twice as many dishes and knives and forks as we could possibly put in the small apartment we had rented.

I went outside when I heard the Coast Guard helicopter hovering just offshore. From our street I could see glimpses of some emergency vehicles parked along the cliffs, so I walked down to see what was happening. A crowd of people were milling around in front Annie's parents' house, and I could make out a few figures picking their way over the cliff face off to the south.

A small boat, the kind used for lifesaving, was manoeuvring just beyond the surf line, and a few guys on surfboards were paddling down from a place where it's easier to get in. Somebody had a bullhorn out there, somebody was waving in the air. "... about ten feet down," an amplified voice floated above the sound of the waves.

"There's a little kid missing," one of the cops said when I asked. "Lives over there," he added, pointing to Annie's house. "Must have wandered away."

"Do you need somebody to go down the cliff?" I asked back immediately. Yes, I'm sure I didn't hesitate, that I knew what I had to do.

More amplified words drifted up from the small boat. "Do they see the kid?'" I asked.

Another man, this one in civilian clothes but with something military about his manner, pointed toward a place where the rock curved abruptly. "Can't tell what it is, but it's the same colour as the sweatshirt the kid had on."

"I'll go take a look," I said. The man with the bullhorn turned toward me, ready to say something, but the voice from boat wavered across the water again. "... moved ..." it said. The attention of everyone swept out to sea, and I was over the barrier and ten feet down the path before anyone glanced my way.

I had not been aware of just how bright or how hot the sun was. The breeze was still blowing, of course. It always blew, that was the reason that all trees, all bushes, all living things leaned away from the ocean. But the sun was trapped here against the cliff, and the wind had to slow down when it reached the rock surface. I smelled the sweetness of the small plants growing in the niches of the rock. I felt my sweat begin to bead under my arms and across my upper lip.

How old had I been the first time I started down this trail. Five? Six? My mother had gone ahead of me, carrying her basket, which she'd bought in Mexico and which matched the sandals she had on and the hat that was supposed to keep the sun off her face.

At the time the trail zigzagged down the pale orange rock. It paused next to the cove where at high tide the waves crashed close enough for their spray to soak the rock. I would want to stop and watch the water roil greenly below, but my mother would hurry me on. "Too dangerous," she'd say. Then, almost to herself, "Maybe this wasn't such a good idea." Always that: maybe this wasn't such a good idea. But she never turned back.

Now I saw that the trail had collapsed into the cove under the weight of all those years and years of beating waves. If the waves rolled in on the average of four a minute, how many would have crashed against the rocks since I was five? Eighteen times 365 times 24 times 60 times 4: 37 million plus change. A small nation of waves, an annual deficit of pounding. No wonder a clutter of rocks now lay at the bottom.

The trail had to climb to get around the place that had caved in, then go down steeply. If the kid had come down this way, he might have had a tricky time getting past. But I saw no sign of recent passage: no slide marks in the loose rock, no crushed plants, no footprints in the places where sand had gathered. I could see, however, what the men in the boat had seen.

Something lying where the rocks flattened out. Light blue, with a darker blue that could be trim or could be shadows. Hard to judge just how big from this distance, but too small to be a child, surely, even a young one.

I slipped at the last step before the trail ended. I went down on one knee and felt the sandstone scrape my skin. Then, as I prepared to stand up, I saw the landscape from a small boy's height. Right here, at the first shelf of rock, was one of the places where my mother liked to work. You could see the fog bank waiting out to sea, the sea stack just to the south, the purple outline of the hills to the north, the golden tones of the rock.

The helicopter was sweeping low over me now. Inside I could see the pilot and someone else peering down at the blue object on the rocks. The machine hovered for a moment, and then lifted sharply up in the air, heading back out to sea.

Once it was gone I rushed forward toward the object, which appeared to have been moved by the helicopter's prop wash. No, I could see it was not a boy, just a sweatshirt. I picked it up and looked at it: small, wet, and with the end of the left sleeve frayed as if someone had chewed on it. Size five, according to the ticket in the back of the neck.

The boy would be what? Four and a half?

Voices roared over the bullhorn. I turned around, waving the sweatshirt over my head.

"... cave ..." I thought I heard.

The man on the cliff with the bullhorn was shouting again. "Get back ... professional ... don't want you to ..." The words floated against the wind and I decided to ignore them. But I saw that two people had started down the trail after him: a man and a woman.

The man was dressed in dark trousers and a dark short-sleeved shirt, so he probably was a policeman, although from this distance it was hard to be sure. The woman was heavy, wearing knee-length shorts and a white sweatshirt or sweater. Impossible for me to tell how old she was, but I saw that her hair was gathered in a braid or a ponytail, which hung down over her shoulder. I thought it might be Annie. I hadn't seen her in such a long, long time.

Seagulls wheeled somewhere: their mewling sounded above the surf. I turned to look at them. The scavengers, the rats of the sea.

But I saw no birds. The sound was coming not from the sky but from just over the edge of the rock to my right.

And there I saw ... I saw ... I had to rub my hands over my face before I could allow myself to look carefully. It was the boy all right, it had to be the boy. Lying in a tide pool, three feet below the main rock shelf on a little spit of rock that glistened with spray. And bent sideways, bent somehow with his legs twisted and his eyes open and his lips trying to say something. Only mewling like a seagull.

But alive.

What to do? What to do? The child was looking at me, but I wasn't sure how much he saw. His clothes were wet: the tide must have come up almost to him, so that the waves splashed him but did not carry him away.

I heard amplified voices again, this time coming from out to sea. I turned to look and saw the boat trying to swing in for a better look.

"... got there?" a voice called through the bullhorn.

"The boy," I shouted back. And then, when I realized that my voice would be lost in the noise of the sea, I waved the sweatshirt in the air with one hand and made a thumb's up sign with the other high above my head.

"Don't try ... move him ... let the professionals ..." the voice called, again breaking up against the background noise.

Yes, of course. You shouldn't move people who may have been seriously injured: spinal cord damage, compound fractures, shock, all the things that the son of a doctor had heard about. But I could go down by the little twisted body, I could tell the child that help was on the way. That would help, comfort always helped.

(And Annie had been the one to comfort me, I should never forget that. She had put her arms around me. She had been the only one.)

The mewling rose in pitch, and now that I was down next to the boy, I could hear his raspy, laboured breathing.

"It's okay, champ. Everything is going to be all right," I said. I kneeled down beside the boy and wondered just where I could touch him and not hurt him.

A helicopter was coming back. I looked up, waiting for the machine to appear overhead so I could signal to it. As I did, I realized that Annie and the man were standing just above me on the edge of the rock.

No, I never wished the boy ill, never wished anything bad for Annie. She had been so sweet, after all. So sweet, so sweet, and how I had loved her!

~

Annie

~

His wife, his little, pretty trophy wife, came to the funeral and wanted to give us her condolences. She talked to me apparently. I don't remember, I'd taken a tranquilizer because I didn't see how I was going to get through the service intact otherwise. I was a zombie, I couldn't even get mad at whatever her name is.

I knew he'd been married once before, Gus told me about the other one, and his two boys, and the good job back east. I didn't dwell on it when he told me; there was no point. I had Chuck and Will and the girls and a job that was interesting part of the time and useful all of the time. My life was pretty damn good, and if I ever felt sorry for myself, all I had to do was look at Gus.

Poor old Gus. For a long time the only thing he had going for him was the fact that he got clobbered doing something he loved. One minute it was a brilliant September morning and he was jumping to his feet on his board. The next thing it's three weeks later, and he's paralyzed from the neck down with a fracture at the fourth cervical vertebra.

I didn't see him during that period, when he just lay there and blamed the universe. Our paths crossed later, when he'd started programming computers and doing his weather stuff and was bringing in enough money to buy all the gadgets invented for guys injured in Vietnam.

We talked a lot then, and he even lived with us for about a year and a half, when Chuck was starting Reed's Garden and wanted me at home to do the bookkeeping and stuff like that. I quit working at the rehab place I'd been and stayed home to do that and manage Gus's care. He paid us what he'd been paying the place he'd been, and we all came out winners. For a while, that is, until we decided that we'd rather be friends. The complex was opening, and he bought in, and I got a job that fit my schedule, and everything was cool.

It catches up with you, doesn't it? You think it's going to be all right. You think that everything finally is turning your way. And it whips around in your hands like a cable come loose in a high wind, and you don't know what it's going to destroy.

Chuck wanted blood. I was surprised by that. Here's a guy who has always been live-and-let-live. Who's a forgiving man — this millennium tour is part truth and reconciliation for him, like those commissions they set up in South Africa and Argentina, to look at the past and then go on. The Vietnam part of the tour was going to be his act of forgiveness.

But he wanted whoever killed Will to suffer.

So did I, I think. I don't know for sure, because I was too out of it to say much. Too much Valium, too much sorrow.

That day in the church with all the people around and the minister talking about a fine young life snuffed out, I know I tried hard to go through the motions. I tried to appear calm, so Meredith and our girls could be strong, so I could think back and remember that I had done the right thing. I even gave Mrs. Rutherford a hug when she came up after the service

The last time I'd seen her, the kids and I had had been out for a walk along the cliffs after a Sunday dinner at my folks. She was walking with Dr. Mercer, and when we came upon them she was telling him something, pointing north and pointing south. In retrospect I imagine they were discussing the park campaign — she was one of the ringleaders for public access and cliff preservation, although all he wanted was to keep out riffraff developers.

"You're blooming," she said to me when I'd introduced her to Chuck and the kids. "You look marvelous, like life is agreeing with you."

I nodded, and added (yes, I'm sure I added), "Thanks for all your help."

But since then I hadn't seen her.

This time, after the songs and prayers and Will's good friends talking about what a good guy he was, the main thing I remember was the way she kept repeating: "It was an accident, it was an accident."

Accidents will happen. Gus had an accident, so did Will when he was little.

But this, this … how can it be an accident? How can you forgive someone who knifes another man for no good reason, not on a dark alley somewhere but early in the morning in the parking lot of a health care facility?

And to learn that this man who killed your son was his father: that is beyond belief.

~

Rick

~

The funeral was December 9, and that afternoon when I called Lil she said she was ready to take all the money that she was going to get from the sale of her house and put it up as a guarantee for my bail. That wouldn't be enough, not even if we added it to whatever Jenny was able to raise from her relatives and the equity we had in Chez Cassis and our house.

It was noisy in the day room, and I had to shout into the phone. "Lil," I said, "you're terrific. But you can't do that. What are you going to live on? You need that money to finance whatever you arrange for yourself."

She made a lot of nice noises about how she'd find a way, but I knew it wouldn't work so there was no point in her trying. "Don't worry, Lil," I said. "It was an accident. They'll come to their senses soon enough."

Yeah, six months from now, which was the soonest we could hope for a trial date, after I'd been held in jail and Cassis's heart had been broken because her father was a criminal, and the restaurant had gone belly-up for lack of my management, and the new century, the new millennium, which we put so much store by, had started with my personal defeat.

But I couldn't say that to her or to Jenny. The least I could do was try to look on the bright side, to channel everything I was feeling — the anger, the guilt, the fear — into finding some creative solution, like Jenny always tells me to do. So I thought and thought, trying to keep my mind off my knee and the other guys in jail with me. The only thing I could come up with was a long shot: trying to get bail reduced.

Now, if you think you've been unfairly treated in your initial bail hearing, you can petition within five days of your arraignment to have it reconsidered. The charges don't come up, there's no chance to present new evidence, the only arguments allowed are those bearing on why the original bail was so high. But maybe, my lawyer said, we could slip in some details that would convince the judge that one, I was trustworthy, and two, the charges were unnecessarily severe.

"Tell me anything that might mean you should be up on a lesser charge, anything that would argue that you would be the last person on earth to have killed this man with malice aforethought," he said.

I considered a minute. "There's all that stuff which I already told the sheriff, how I was exhausted and not thinking straight," I began. We were sitting in the area where prisoners met visitors, with plexiglass between us and telephones to talk into; not the best atmosphere for thinking up strategy.

"It's got to be more than that, because I assume they have seen those police records your wife told me about." The probation report had been right: I'd never been convicted of anything. But twice when I was working in other people's kitchens and I was pushing so hard, the cops got called; like I said at the beginning, people around me were into enhanced performance then, and I was having a hard time keeping up. It wasn't a healthy environment, shall we say.

And — and this is something I probably should have said straight out before, but even now years later I find it hard to think about — there's the reason I had to drive back to Montreal to visit Caroline's boys that first winter I was in Kingston. See, after we had that fight in the Adirondacks when I hurt her, she got a court order to keep me away from them unless she was around. It was three years before I got visiting rights and they could come down and see me. Jenny helped me with that, it's another thing I owe her for. But the boys got out of the habit of having a father, and even now they don't want to spend time with Jenny, Cassis, and me.

Neither of these are things I'm proud of, but they're things I know I should admit to. It's just that I've put them behind me, I've risen above them.

"And there is the matter of the pills," the lawyer was saying. "You may be a solid citizen, but with them in your pocket it looks like you spent part of your time solidly stoned."

"No, no, they were in my pocket because I had nothing to hide," I told him. "If I did use drugs, I would have hidden them at Lil's place."

He shook his head when I said that, but made a few notes, anyway. "No, what I really need is a convincing argument that you are a victim in this too. The knee injury might help, you need better medical treatment than you can get here. And with some other element, we might be able to get bail down where you could think about paying it." He looked at his watch, his time was up. "Give me a call if you have any ideas."

I nodded, and let them lead me away. I couldn't think of anything then, because it hurt so much to walk. It was only when I was stretched out on my bunk, trying to massage the knee into some sort of equilibrium that I realized the answer.

A man doesn't knowingly kill his son. I am in mourning too.

Jenny didn't know about Annie's boy. Even when I started to clean up my life, to take responsibility for my actions the way she says I should and all that, I just couldn't say anything about Annie, and about her kid. It had been a secret for so long, all my life had been built on it.

But I recognize that I should have told Jenny. Actually I was planning to do it soon, because she had been after me to write a new will, now that Caroline's boys were pretty well grown and we'd acquired more property. I changed things a bit when Jenny and I got married, but that was both before my father died, and before Cassis was born. The restaurant wasn't mentioned anywhere, and if there's anything that Jenny should get were I to die it would be that. She's worked so hard, she believes in my dreams.

And when my father died Caroline's boys were the big inheritors. He left me my mother's watercolours, and some stock that had been hers, but aside from the trust he'd set up for Lil everything went to Richie and Matt. Some of it is in trust until they're twenty-five, and some of it is earmarked for their educations, but they're going to be well-off young men. So I don't need to provide for them.

It's a different story for Annie's son, it was a different story, I mean. I should have seen that he got something, a watercolour by my mother at the very least. And if I made that change in my will I would have had to tell Jenny why I was doing it.

But I had resisted doing it. Because of cowardice, I guess.

Might have beens, might have beens. What I had to do was decide if it was worth doing now.

I tried to get Jenny to give me some straight answers about what was happening with Chez Cassis. Running a restaurant is such a balancing act, it's the details that make the difference, not only in getting the food on the table, but also in making sure that you come in on budget. I cared, I'd track down the best stuff around, and I'd make sure that none of it was wasted. Would anybody else?

I decided to call Gus to see what he thought. He hadn't tried to contact me directly, true, but from what Jenny said he'd said at the funeral, he wanted me to get a message. I'd tell him that nobody else knew as much, or was as wise as he was. My friend for all these years, he'd help me.

~

Annie

~

S*ecrets, secrets. If I had it to* do over again, I would never have kept anything secret. Telling the truth at the beginning has its consequences, but if someone knows something hidden about you, they have power over your for the rest of your life.

On the weekend after the funeral, Gus called me up. He said he'd been trying to get through since right after Will died, but that Chuck or the girls said I wasn't in any shape to talk to anyone. That was right, and actually Chuck was out or I probably wouldn't have answered the phone that day. But I thought the phone call might be from Meredith, and I hadn't talked to her at all privately. At the funeral I couldn't even look her in the eye, poor sweetheart. *Maybe*, I thought, as I lay in bed listening to the ring, *I should ask her and her boy over for Christmas*. Will had said they'd be by sometime during the holiday, but we hadn't set a date yet. It would be nice to see her little boy …

I figured it was Gus as soon as I picked up the receiver because he uses a speakerphone, and you immediately know it's not a regular call since you can hear what's going on in the room where he is.

"Hello, Annie-baby, when are you coming back to work? We miss you," he said without saying his name. His voice is unmistakable: deep, but since he is on a respirator part of the time, his lung function makes it not much louder than a whisper.

"And good afternoon to you, Gus," I said. "I hope you're feeling well." There are times when he is blunter than most people, he always says he has to make every minute count, but I was in no shape to be rushed into a serious conversation.

He paid no attention to my chit-chat. "When are you coming back?" he asked again.

I didn't answer immediately. Until then I hadn't faced the question head-on. I knew that the people at the complex had told Chuck they expected me to take time off, it was clear they were going to be pretty decent about it all. But how could I go back there now?

"I don't know," I said. "Maybe never, maybe I'll just change jobs." There are always ads for people like me, all I'd have to do is call the personnel director at a couple of other places and the word would get out. "You can't," he said, before I could explain. "We need you."

He didn't add, "I need you." That was good. Back when he was staying with us, that had been the problem, not that we ever talked about it. Paralysis doesn't do anything to a man's desire for women, even if it removes the ability to act on it in the usual manner. I knew that, I'd changed enough quadriplegics and paraplegics who had wet dreams or huge erections. One or two of them cried because there was no pleasure in the experience, not even in their dreams. But when Gus was staying with us and began to have them every night, unbidden and unwanted, I knew that what was going on in his head was more complicated than mere friendship. He needed me, he thought. He wanted me, but I could not oblige him. Since he moved to the complex I did a lot of things for him, but the schedule was arranged so that much of his personal care was done by others, and I'd suggested that the others be changed frequently so he wouldn't get too attached to them either. The desire to love, or just simple desire, is so much a part of you and me and everyone. It leads us where we might not go if we were thinking with our heads and not our hormones.

But that is old news. I stopped myself from travelling further on that train of thought. "Give me time," I told Gus. "I can't face the place right now."

"Could I talk to you, though?" he asked.

"Aren't we talking now?"

"No, I mean face to face. What about meeting at the beach at Encinitas tomorrow afternoon?"

"Why?"

"I want to talk to you."

"Should I bring Chuck? I don't much feel like driving these days."

There was a sharp intake of air. "No," he said. "Don't do that. Come by yourself. You wouldn't want anybody else there."

The beach was not far from where we lived. Our house was next to Reed's Garden Experts on fifteen acres bought when the land around here wasn't nearly as expensive as it is now, and Chuck could afford enough to grow some of the plants he used. That was back when the area still had fields of poinsettias and bulbs and cut flowers, and the famous Japanese family vegetable garden that's written up in all the gourmet magazines was just a truck farm with a stand by the side of the road. Since then the countryside has disappeared under houses. We'd be millionaires if Chuck ever sold our land.

But the beaches belong to everyone. There's a point break where Gus said to meet him, and since I got there before he did, I sat in my car and watched three guys on surfboards, trying their luck in the sloppy surf left by the first winter storm. The air was thick with spray and low clouds so I couldn't see beyond the second line of breakers, but that was enough.

The water looked cold, and when I got out of my car to greet Gus when he arrived in his adapted minivan the air was cold too. His driver thought he was nuts to get out, but he insisted that he wanted to feel the mist on his face. "I get tired of the same temperature, the same humidity all the time," he said. "I need to experience the elements every once in a while."

And he rolled down to the edge of the parking lot, where we could look out over the waves. "I take it as a measure of my maturity that I can watch those guys out there without either dying of envy or freaking out in fear for what might happen to them," he said to me.

I had a raincoat on that sort of flapped around me, and the wind blew his words from his mouth so I had to bend over close to him so I could both hear him and wrap the raincoat around me to keep warm. "That's a complete recovery in one sense," I said. And I thought it was: he'd made a good thing of his life against terrible odds. "You know I think you're one of the world's greatest success stories."

He laughed, a funny laugh that's choked off because he can't get a big lungful of air behind it. "Those were the days, though. Back when I was king of the beach."

"Yeah," I said, grinning because it was so long ago and we'd been so stupid with youth. "You were the reincarnation of the Great Kahuna."

"And you were Gidget and it was an endless summer, one continual beach party, and ..."

"I was never Gidget," I retorted. "Gidget was the algebra type, and Mrs. Rutherford always saw that I got in advanced math ..."

He cut me off before I could go on. "That's what I wanted to talk to you about. What happened back then. Back when things were golden."

Golden? He's done so well, but still he can't get free of the past, I thought. But as I listened to what he was trying to explain I saw just how deep the past was buried in us all, like a broken hook festering in a fish who got away, but only for a while.

R.J. wanted to talk to me, Gus said, and to do so I should go to his lawyer's office this afternoon, right away.

"You're kidding me? Why doesn't he talk to me himself?"

"That's the problem," Gus said. "He wants to, but he can't come see you to plead his case. He's in jail, remember. He can't even have visitors except family and his lawyer. But he can call out, and he's going to do just that — place a call to his lawyer — in half an hour and he's hoping you'll be there."

I turned away from him and looked back out at the ocean. One of the surfers had caught a wave just right, and was moving and moving so that he ran down the face of the wave southward, spinning a long ride by clever footwork, turning a moment of exhilaration into a heart-stopping run.

There was no reason why I should do anything to help R.J. I didn't owe him diddly-squat. "Chuck thinks he deserves the death penalty," I said.

"R.J. told me to tell you that you should remember who found Will."

Yes, there was that.

"And his stepmother, who was Mrs. Rutherford, remember, she's concerned, he says."

"What does she know?" I asked, turning around sharply. My father was dead, so was Dr. Mercer, and my mother thought mostly about her childhood these days. I hoped no one else had been told about Will and R.J. and me.

"She doesn't know the whole story, she just thinks this is a tragic accident — and these are her words — 'which links two people of whom I am very fond.'"

"R.J. and me?" I shook my head, thinking of those days R.J. and I worked on English assignments together for her class. "I don't want to talk about that," I said. "But she hasn't changed, has she? She still won't end a sentence with a preposition."

Gus did not laugh. "Yeah," he said. He turned his wheelchair to have a better view of the surfers. Two of them were up now, riding the break south, shifting every few seconds to keep their boards riding slantwise down the face of the wave. One pulled up as the wave hit the bottom and began to lose its force. But the other jigged slightly and skillfully to get another three seconds of ride. "Nice," Gus said. "One of my regrets is that I will never get to see what I could do on one of the new boards."

One of my regrets, I suddenly realized, was that R.J. and I never had that last, necessary conversation. Dr. Mercer hadn't wanted it, and then R.J. had avoided it. But maybe this was the time. "All right," I said to Gus. "Let's go. I'll talk to him. But not with the lawyer present."

The lawyer didn't like that idea, nor did the trophy wife, who was hovering in the office when we arrived. "I thought you said they didn't know what R.J. wants to talk to me about?" I said to Gus after I had insisted they leave the room.

"He said they don't," Gus said, but he sounded a little doubtful too. "I wouldn't have agreed to set this up otherwise, even for old time's sake."

Old time's sake! Hah, I thought, but nevertheless when the phone rang I did what Gus told me to do so the call could come in on the speakerphone. And then it was too late.

You must remember that I had not heard R.J.'s voice in nearly thirty years, since that day on the cliffs. It had been even longer since we'd talked on the phone. I hadn't seen his picture in the newspapers or on TV because Chuck and the girls hid the papers and kept me from watching the news during those awful days after Will died, but I knew he must be going soft and grey like all men his age. A glimpse of him wouldn't have affected me, I'm sure. But I wasn't prepared for his voice.

"Hello, Annie," he said with just the same hint of softness that I remembered from those long telephone conversations we had had. The timbre was deeper, maybe a little rougher: living does that to you. But I would have recognized his voice anywhere. All those looping, lazy conversations on the phone while we did our homework, those walks along Sunset Cliffs, his whispers in my ear as we lay together under the fragrant bushes.

Then, suddenly another memory surged upward unbidden: an afternoon back in our house, in Chuck's and my house, the one that Chuck built for us. Will was sixteen and sitting on the floor in the living room with his school books on the coffee table in front of him, the way I used to study when I waited for R.J. This time Will was talking on the phone — times had changed, everyone had phones in every room by then — but I heard him speaking just as softly, as intimately as R.J. always spoke to me. I don't know who the girl was — it doesn't matter, Will had several when he was in high school, he was twenty before we would see him with the same face more than once — but it was clear he was filled with the same mixture of innocence and longing that I remembered from R.J.

The light was fading, and Will didn't notice me for a minute or two as I stood in the shadow of the doorway. Then perhaps I moved or the floor creaked — my house doesn't have my mother's wall-to-wall carpet — and he sensed I was there. He looked up quickly, almost furtively, and I saw on his narrow face and in his grey-green eyes the same wariness I remembered from those moments when R.J. spoke about his father and his mother.

"Got to go," Will said to the girl on the phone. "I'm being spied on."

"No, you're not," I said after he cut the connection. "I just was coming in to turn on the lights."

He looked at me steadily for a moment before he grinned and stretched. "Sure, sure, they all say that," he said. "When's supper? I'm going to meet her later anyway."

There have been many times when I have been overcome with tenderness for Chuck and my children, when something they've done has plunged directly into my heart and stirred my feelings so that I've had to hold on tight to whatever was close to hand. But this was the only time after the days of surfing Ocean Beach that the love I had once felt for the boy who had fathered this boy flared up again. It was mixed with regret, and also with fear for what Will might become. *Let him not be like R.J.*, I prayed. But at the same time I knew that I was lucky to have Will for a son.

"Hello," I said to his father, to this stranger who had killed my son but who still claimed a place — a tiny, secret, hidden place — in my heart.

"In case Gus didn't tell you, I want to clear anything I say with you," R.J. began. "I mean, how could I …?"

He left the question hanging in the air, and I felt my defences crumble a little more. I could almost see him as he was all those years ago. That entire summer I had imagined what it would be like if he suddenly appeared — walked into the bakery where I was working, came by my parents' house, called and asked me to meet him somewhere. I loved him, God how I loved him. I would have dumped Danny no matter what agreement my mother and Dr. Mercer had reached.

But of course he didn't call, he didn't even write.

So I interrupted: "What is it that you want?"

He didn't say anything for a moment. I heard him swallow and clear his throat. "I want to come clean," he said. He paused, like he was waiting for my reaction, but when I didn't say anything, he went on. "I want to acknowledge my mistakes and praise you for all you did, raising a fine son and all that. I want to tell how I went looking for him that time that he disappeared on the cliffs. And I want to say that killing him was a terrible accident that I will weigh me down for the rest of my life."

He paused again, like he wanted me to say, "Go on, go on," but I couldn't speak because the feelings twisting inside me took my breath away.

He must have thought my silence was agreement. "If I do, I might be able to get out on bail," he said. "Otherwise, this terrible accident is going to ruin everything for me and those around me. We're going to lose our restaurant. My little girl, my sweet little girl …" His voice got thick, he choked, he seemed unable to go on.

What would have happened if he had just said, "I'm sorry for what I did, I can never repent enough, but you know I never would have done such a horrible thing on purpose? Please don't make things worse, please don't ruin the rest of my life."

I don't know, and he didn't say that, and when he mentioned his daughter I thought of my own girls and of Chuck, and how they would be hurt by R.J.'s confessions. Imagine what supermarket weeklies could do with the story — Man kills love child three decades later: Greek tragedy in San Diego County.

And what they would think of me for being deceitful all those years?

"Stop it," I said. "Do you think you can get out of the murder charge by confessing that you were a coward more than thirty years ago? Don't you think it is about time you grew up?"

"It's true about finding him that time," he answered back. "I did, you know I did, he was just lying there on the rocks and the tide might have got him, and where were you when it happened. Why weren't you taking better care of him?"

I had been working. My mother was babysitting Will the way she had since we moved back and I started the LVN course. We were going to move soon, though, because I had started a good job a few weeks before and I figured I'd have enough together in two months so we could rent a decent place.

But in the meantime we slept in my old room, and ate with my parents, and Will knew he wasn't supposed to go any further than the stretch of sidewalk between our two neighbours' driveways. He knew he shouldn't cross Sunset Cliffs without someone grown-up with him, and until that afternoon I don't think he ever did. But he was four and a bit then, big for his age, and that morning (he said later) he saw a rabbit on the other side of the road. He said he looked both ways before crossing the way everyone said he should. And then he ran after the bunny ...

My mother was doing something inside, and when she checked about 11:00 A.M. to see what he was doing, he was gone. She called his name, but when he didn't jump out from behind the bushes by the side of the house, or emerge laughing from one of the cars parked in the driveway, she began by knocking on neighbours' doors to see if he'd gone visiting. An hour later she had everybody out looking. An hour after that the police were breaking out their emergency search plan, and my mother called me at work.

I wanted to search too, I wanted to go out with the groups who were elbow to elbow on the cliffs, looking behind every big rock and into each wave-carved slit. But the rescue captain told me not to, told me that I would be needed when they found Will and that I should keep myself for that. Which meant as the afternoon wore on and the search became more serious — helicopters, surfers checking out the rocks from the sea, divers getting ready to look in the deep holes off the furthest rocks — I could do nothing but pace up and down along the road overlooking the cliffs.

I did not see R.J, arrive, and I didn't recognize Gus and his friends on their boards, either. But when the helicopter swept in I did see a man on the far bench of rocks who was waving madly in the air. I knew immediately what he saw and I took off running as fast as I could.

There are three people who knew who found Will: Gus (whom I told one of those midnights when we sat up on the ward), myself, and R.J. But then I had no idea who the guy kneeling beside my boy was, I just tried to move him out of the way so I could hold Will's hand, while I prayed that the rescue staff would do something quick about the pain that was making my baby cry. Only when the medics had started work and I moved out of their way did I realize the man was still standing beside me.

"What the hell was the kid doing out on the cliffs by himself?" he said.

I looked around. What kind of question was that? I suspected I would be asking it myself later when this ordeal was all over, but for the moment I didn't want to hear it from anybody else.

Then I saw who it was. A little older, of course, with longer hair and glasses, but R.J. without a doubt. "How'd you get here?" was all I could say.

He shrugged. "I joined the search. I'm back for a few days," he said. "Who was supposed to be looking after the kid?" There was an edge to his voice, like he had a right to ask.

I might have said something then, but two of the rescue crew came running up with a special stretcher. We had to move even further back, and so we stood with nothing to do but pray.

"Who was supposed to be looking after the kid?" R.J. asked again.

I didn't answer: Will began screaming at whatever the medics were doing. "Mommy's here," I said, trying to project my voice straight into my baby's ears. "Mommy's here. It's going to be all right."

I stretched out my arms, I wanted to hold him, but R.J. pulled me back roughly. "And that's the way you take care of this child."

I turned to face him. "Who are you to judge? Where have you been all his life?" For a long moment we stared at each other.

That would have been the moment for him to do the right thing, to become something to Will. It would have been easy: he was a hero for finding Will, for Christ's sake.

But he dropped his gaze. He turned away. He didn't give his name to the police or the lifeguard squad, the news stories talked about the mystery rescuer.

He walked out again. He blew it.

Now he was saying: "You weren't the perfect mother, don't forget. What about that time in the mountains? That race where the guy got killed? I heard …"

"I left Danny over that, remember. I made a better life for us."

He didn't say anything immediately. I could hear the noises in the day room he was calling from, someone whistling, the rumble of the television, a man swearing gleefully about something.

"Oh Annie, Annie, Annie," he said finally. "I don't know … what a mess this is …"

"Yes, it is," I said, and hung up.

Then I left, not saying a thing to the lawyer or to the trophy wife when I passed them in the outer office. Gus rolled after me, but I didn't want to talk to him either. The fact is I didn't know what to say.

When I got home there was no one there yet, and I went in the bathroom to wash my face. I looked at myself in the mirror and saw what was left of the girl I had been, the overweight woman with light brown hair that used to bleach nearly blonde in the summer but now was sprinkled with grey. Hair that Will and both my girls had too, something that I had given to them along with a certain amount of security and a lot of love.

I started to cry then. I cried and I cried and I cried, the way I might have after the funeral if I hadn't been frozen by the pills everyone said I should take.

By the time Chuck came home, I'd made my decision. I didn't care what R.J. did. Let him tell the world whatever he wanted. With Will dead, there was no connection between us.

My life was elsewhere. I'd take my chances with the people who loved me now.

"Listen," I said when Chuck and I were in the kitchen, having a beer while the pizza for supper was heating in the oven "You haven't done anything about those tickets, have you?"

"For the trip?" he asked. He looked sheepish. "No," he said. "I faxed my friend in Sydney to say that we might have to postpone it, but I was waiting until you wanted to talk about it before I did anything definite."

We were scheduled to leave in less than two weeks. That would be all right, I didn't want to wait around to see what R.J. did. "Good," I said. "I want to go."

He looked at me carefully, assessing me, wondering if what he was hearing was the rambling of a woman who still was not quite functioning. "You're sure?" he said. "You don't think it would be too much?" There was a little lilt to his voice, though. He was glad to hear what I had to say.

"Yes, I'm sure. If I'm going to grieve, I don't want to grieve here." Then I willed myself to go on to the next thing. "Maybe we ought to take the girls and Meredith and her boy, too, at least as far as New Zealand," I said. "For New Year's."

"It might be hard to get tickets at this late date, and besides, it would cost a fortune," he began, but I could hear that he liked the idea.

"So? What else do we have to go in debt for?"

After we'd seen the fireworks and Maori dancing in Wellington, after we'd watched the sun come up over the Pacific Ocean for the first time in the new year, new century, new millennium, after the young folks had gone back to California, I told Chuck about R.J.

We were walking along a beach near Sydney, looking at the ocean crash against this shore, far away from our ordinary lives, yet connected.

Our trip was half over. There had been no word from home about progress in the case, no indication that R.J. had made any revelations in an attempt to make things easier for himself. And Will had been with us in spirit all along. I'd see his smile on the face of another young man, there'd be the roar of a motorcycle and I'd look up expecting to see him. Or the girls and Meredith would tell a story about something he'd done — sometimes funny, often kind. And twice a day at least I'd catch myself wondering what he would think about something we were seeing, telling myself to remember the details of the beach or the pub or the gardens so I would be able to describe them to him.

Chuck didn't say anything immediately after I'd finished with all the sad story — R.J. and me, Dr. Mercer and my mother, Danny and the pickup. Will, always Will. Chuck's hands were in his pockets and he jingled his keys as he walked. I didn't touch him because I wanted him to make up his mind on his own.

Then, looking out across the ocean, he said he wished I hadn't worried so much about telling him. He said he hated R.J. all the more. But, he said, we could live with all that.

~

Rick

~

M*y eyes are closed but I can* see the light. The sun is there still, hanging three hours from sunset above the ocean. The inner sides of my eyelids are the golden orange of fruit or flowers or flames.

My ears are filled by the wind, and behind that sound, I hear the waves and then, like the bass line in a song, the much nearer beat of my heart, of my blood rushing through my ears.

There is a smell, which is both sweet and bitter. Part of it is the saltiness from the sea. Part of it is the bushes that cover the cliffs along here. The smell is part of the wind, is part of the season, is part of me.

Lil died last week, and Jenny and I are back on the coast to see her buried and her things taken care of. She never did move out of the house, the final papers never got signed; she had to pay a big penalty to the people who wanted to buy it, but that's what she said she wanted. She got by for nearly two more years with someone coming in every day to help her with her meals. Then at the very end she spent a week and a half in the hospital. When we talked her on the phone, she told us not to come: she said she'd be going home soon.

Keeping the house was very convenient for us, because it meant that Jenny and Cassis had someplace to stay when I was in jail. In all, Jenny came out five times during those seven months, and Cassis was there for Christmas and Easter vacation.

We didn't ask for a bail review. After Annie hung up on me at the lawyer's office I decided there wasn't any point: better to put our money in a good defence team than try to bail me out. Lil helped us pay the lawyers, bless her. She said she owed it to my father, and I decided not to remind her how little my father thought of me.

And I got off, in a manner of speaking. It was an accident, of course, and the judge reduced the charge at the preliminary hearing to involuntary manslaughter. We did a little back and forth, a kind of plea bargain, and well before I'd ordinarily come to trial, I pleaded guilty, and the judge sentenced me to the time I'd already spent in jail. I was back in Kingston, picking up the pieces at Chez Cassis, before the summer season was well underway.

And, no, I never did make my relation to William Wallace Reed public. I realized that the man I wanted to be wouldn't do that. But after it was all over I told Jenny, because, like I said, I was going to eventually, sometime.

"So that's what happened in that lawyer's office," she said when I finally explained. We were sitting on the terrace at Chez Cassis, looking out through the trees toward the Hudson, late on the first Sunday night after I'd come home. The restaurant had operated at a loss all through the spring, but it had operated. All that business over the New Year had given us a little cushion, so even though we were deeper in debt, it could have been worse. "I thought you just wanted to make something of the fact that Lil had been so good to Mrs. Reed."

Mrs. Reed: I'd never thought of Annie that way. But that's who she was.

"No," I said. I was tired, I hadn't worked in a kitchen for months, and my hands had lost their toughness and my muscles, their strength. The only thing that improved about me was my knee, which got better when I was in jail: benign neglect, the orthopaedic surgeon said when he saw it. All that lying around with nothing to do. I flexed my leg as I sat with Jenny, realizing that even after ten hours on my feet, it didn't hurt. "No, I was getting prepared to do something a whole lot weaker and more immature than just mentioning that Lil wrote a letter of recommendation once upon a time."

I paused, and Jenny reached out and took my right hand — greasy with the vitamin E cream I'd put on the places where I'd been burned by hot pans. "Annie told me to grow up, you know," I said. "Maybe I have. Finally."

Gus came to Lil's funeral. He said that Annie was working someplace else now, and that Chuck had spun off a company that designed special mini-gardens. Reed's Garden Experts still did a lot of lawn mowing and ordinary garden maintenance, but this business let him make miniature landscapes. "There was a big story on him in the paper a couple of months ago," Gus said after. "He talks to you and finds out what you like, what the high points of your life have been and all that, and then he brings together the plants which present a portrait of you. Expensive but very nice, I understand."

I nodded. "Good for him," I said, because that seemed to be the right thing to say. But I didn't want to talk about him or Annie.

"He's doing one for the complex for free though," Gus was saying. "He convinced the board of directors to dig up an area about nine feet square in the middle of the parking lot. A memorial, right where Will was found."

"Good for him," I repeated. A memorial, of course. Should I offer to make a contribution? Even if the design was free, the materials would cost something. We were still operating in the red — post 9/11 and the IT meltdown hasn't been good for upscale places like Chez Cassis — but I could probably scare up a little. Or Lil's estate could.

Jenny came over before I had a chance to offer. "It's good of you to come," she said to Gus. Then she turned to me and held out her hand. "Give that to me," she said.

I looked down: I was playing with my penknife. It was the Épinal she'd bought me last Christmas to replace the other one, the one that killed Will. I carried this one in my pocket now and used it six or eight times a day.

A cook has to use knives.

But, as I do these days when she asks, I handed it to her, because I know you can't be too careful with some things. We want no more accidents.

But perhaps it is true, as Lil said, that you can go home again. Like a magic door in a story, there may come a time when you touch your heart and home opens up before you. It will always be afternoon, three hours before sunset. The wind will always blow, carrying with it the sound of the surf and the smell of the hillside.

My mother will be sitting at the edge of the tide pool, painting a watercolour that captures the intensity of blue sky and blue sea. Lil will be rowing the length of the calanque toward her English officer and the air will be fragrant with thyme. A small boy will kneel beside a burrow in the cliffside, waiting for a bunny to come out, while beyond the breakers a young man shouts with pleasure as he paddles for a wave.

And Annie and R.J. will love each other enough not to make the mistakes they made before.

~

Acknowledgements

~

Thanks to David Homel and Marilyn Laurence for their suggestions on how to tell the story; to San Diego County Sheriff Deputy Laura Heilig, San Diego County Deputy District Attorney Bob Phillips, and Paul Williams of Vista Bail Bonds for information about what happens when someone stabs someone; to Paul Vadnais for the names of surfing beaches I couldn't remember; and to Wallace W. Zane, whose Master's thesis "Surfers of Southern California: Structures of Identity" (1992 McGill University) was a completely unexpected treasure trove of lore. But most of all this book is in memory of my sister Laurie, who never told our mother she surfed.